CW00549670

# A Myth For Dragonflies

**The Dragonfly Series, Volume 1**

Kurt Smith

Published by Kurt Smith, 2023.

A MYTH FOR DRAGONFLIES

**First edition. November 14, 2023.**

Copyright © 2023 Kurt Smith.

ISBN: 979-8223869948

Written by Kurt Smith.

Right out the gate let's just go ahead and classify this story as a piece of fiction. Okay? I'd even go so far as to call it *historical* fiction—you know, a fictional story based on historical facts and whatnot? But nothing remotely close to a piece of historical scholarship. So, for example, it's true that Gouverneur Morris was a historical person, the guy who is said to have penned the *Constitution* of the United States of America, who enjoyed one awesome pegleg and who just so happened to accidentally off himself by trying to unblock a kidney stone or some such by sticking a long needle-shaped whale bone up his you know what. That guy. Both the pegleg and whale bone are in the story, but you'll find no mention of the bit about what he did with that whale bone. Ephraim Hart was also a historical person. He migrated from Franconia, Germany to the New World just before the American Revolution. He was Jewish. His wife was named Frances and his kid named Joel. He was a signatory of the Buttonwood Agreement, the 1792 covenant between New York stockjobbers that laid the groundwork for the New York Stock Exchange. Yeah, that's all in the story, but I'd be really surprised if any of what I say here is true, or if Hart ever did any of the silly things he is depicted doing. This is a sweet, tearjerking comedy. Any historical items are just stage setting—capeesh? It's all made up, except maybe for the underlying philosophical themes. Those, as you will see, seem true enough. I'm hoping you can see that I'm trying to avoid any confusion but more importantly any future lawsuits. Enjoy this entertaining but almost completely fake story.

Yours Truly,
Your Humble but Probably Fictional Narrator

# 1

And so it was in the spring of 1792, when under a buttonwood tree at 68 Wall Street they gathered. And lo twenty-four douches stood like statues wrapped in black wool coats and buckled leather shoes, and though none would swear to it under oath, they would proclaim to anyone who would lend an earhole that the ground beneath them had trembled.

And it was on this day of May that the twenty-four bound themselves by sacred covenant:

> We the Subscribers, Brokers for the Purchase and Sale of the Public Stock, do hereby solemnly promise and pledge ourselves to each other, that we will not buy or sell from this day for any person whatsoever, any kind of Public Stock, at least than one quarter of one percent Commission on the Specie value and that we will give preference to each other in our Negotiations. In Testimony whereof we have set our hands this 17th day of May at New York, 1792.

How Masonic! But Masonic or no, this was the *actual* covenant. Look it up if you don't believe me. From the Buttonwood Agreement, as it would be called, *The New York Stock & Exchange Board* was born. Did you know that? I didn't think so.

Now, the glorious twenty-four did not choose this name right away, but would give it to themselves the 8th of March 1817, one score and five years *after* the gathering under the buttonwood tree. It should probably be added, just to be clear, that in 1863, smack dab in the middle of the Civil War, the name would be changed again, this time to the *New York Stock Exchange*.

But behold—In addition to the twenty-four bound by covenant, there stood on curbs those who also sold stocks and bonds, or *scripts* as they were then called. The twenty-four of the Buttonwood Agreement did not like these guys, and relocated to a tight dank room, where they, still bound by sacred covenant, worked, having to sell a boatload of stocks and bonds, since they were now paying quite a bit a year in rent. It was located at 40 Wall Street. I hope that you can see where this is going. I mean, Wall Street—*Hello?* This is how the entire thing got started.

And behold a smidge further if you will—The parties would further isolate themselves from one another, those guys on the curb remaining on the curb, and those glorious twenty-four who had gathered under the buttonwood tree fleeing to the Tontine Coffee House of all places, located on the North-West corner of Wall Street and Water Street. They, the twenty-four who had gathered under the buttonwood tree, paid no rent to the Tontine Coffee House, which was a sweet deal. But they did have to buy coffee if they wanted to hang out. So they did.

This great divide of the two Holy Cabals took place in the year 1793, not one year having passed since the glorious twenty-four had gathered under the buttonwood tree.

Jealous of the glorious twenty-four who had gathered, jealous of their sacred covenant, jealous of their clever move to the Tontine Coffee House, not to mention of the future fancy name they would eventually give to themselves, it came to pass that those curb-standers would also give to themselves a name. It was something like an act of revenge against the glorious twenty-four. They chose: *The New York Curb Market*. Seriously, that was the name they chose. The lameness was too much for some, and subsequently they changed the name to *The New York Curb Exchange*. Another swing and miss. And it was thrice they would name themselves, three being a magical number, and it would be in 1953 that The New York Curb Exchange would rename itself *The American Stock Exchange*.

And so it was that the two American Holy Cabals, the New York Stock Exchange, and the American Stock Exchange, were conceived.

You're welcome.

# 2

"Usury?" Ephraim Hart asked. "This of which we speak is not usury."

"To charge interest on that which is loaned; is not that usury?" Sheikh Yusuf replied. He, as a matter of fact, had been named after *the* Sheikh Yusuf, which would have been a big deal to Muslims of his mother's generation.

"You are confusing apples with oranges, Sir," Hart insisted. "I lend not money and then burden you with interest. I agree, to do *that* would be usury. But I don't do that."

"To lend *not*-money you say?...Come again!" Yusuf interrupted.

"Come again I shall. Hear this, you jackass—first off, I am not saying that I am lending *not-money*. Who says that? One cannot lend a privation. This, as you surely know, is distinct from someone's *not lending* something. I know that this lending a privation business is exactly how you would like me to construe my words, for as such they would be subject to great metaphysical criticism. Rather, I say that I am neither lending money nor demanding interest. The logic of the negative operates over the entire proposition."

Yusuf's eyes began to glaze over just a bit.

"Thus," Hart continued, "the assertion is *I lend money and demand interest*. And the negation of *that* is what I assert. I am claiming that it is not the case that I lend money and demand interest. Got it? I sell stock. That's what I do. When you buy stock from me, you pay for that service. Sheesh. When did you become such an idiot?"

"You're the idiot." Yusuf leaned forward close enough to now catch a whiff of Hart's floral and musk pomade. "Does it not say in your Holy Book, Sir, that *thou shalt not lend upon usury to thy brother; usury of money, usury of victuals, usury of any thing that is lent upon usury*? Notice that I recite the words accurately. Does it not say what I say it says?"

"Holy Book?" Hart asked. The exchange had entered new territory.

"In *my* Holy Book, it is written: *Those who charge usury are in the same position as those controlled by the Devil's influence.* The Devil's influence, Sir! And that is just in the book of *Al-Baqarah.* There is more where that came from."

"That will be enough of the Holy Books. Observe, you dimwit, charging a fee for providing a service is *not* usury." Hart's face reddened. His left eyelid twitched ever so slightly. "Had you looked a couple of verses further, supposing that we looked again at the Holy Book at which I just forbid you to further look—*my* Holy Book, mind you, not yours—you would have read these the following words: *Unto a stranger thou mayest lend upon usury; but unto thy brother thou shalt not lend upon usury.* So, even though I am *not* doing it in your case, I *may* do it to you if I so desired."

"Offended I am! You consider me a *stranger*?" Yusuf said grievingly.

"Well, you are no Jew, unlike me who is one, and I'm pretty sure that this is the relation to which the word *brother* is referring in the passage you quoted."

Just then, the eyeballs of three men sitting at a table cater-cornered from theirs directed themselves in Hart's direction, this upon their hearing the word "Jew". Interestingly, the eyeballing had not transpired upon Hart's earlier utterance of the word "Muslim," their taking Hart in all likelihood to have been calling his bearded interlocutor a luxuriously woven cotton fabric originating in Bangladesh.

The scene hung there for a moment, as though chiseled in stone, the inhabitants of the two tables locked in a fit of eyeballing.

"Of the Buttonwood Agreement I am so vested," Hart said to the three strangers. Five eyeballs in all were attributable to the three men—one eyeball was wooden, so in Aristotelian fashion, given its unfunctionableness, it was not an eyeball proper, as it is said—so "eyeball" was being used only homonymously with respect to the wooden jobber.

Upon their hearing Hart, their eyeballs returned to the conversation from whence they came, though the wooden one lagged just a bit.

Hart returned to Yusuf. "I claim only my due of a two hundredth part of one hundred percent of the specie value of the stock I sold to you. Bankers may commit the sin of usury, Sir, but not I."

"Ask any ghostly Arian in this den of thieves what I am, Sir, and he shall no doubt tell you that I am just as much a descendant of Abraham as you yourself," Yusuf said with some umph. He paused and looked upward. Then he continued, "A two hundredth part of one hundred percent? What kind of mathematics is this? Do you mean two percent?"

"Maybe," Hart confessed, "Perhaps the amount is what you say. Two percent sounds right."

"Two percent isn't so bad," Yusuf said, "and if that is what you demand, I'm happy to pay it." Hart's face softened. Yusuf continued, "Though not a Jew, I *am* your brother, and therefore no stranger. Biologicals mean something, do they not?"

"*Half* brother," Hart corrected. "But," now whispering with some ferocity to avoid any further eyeballing, "as far as the *brother* reference is concerned, to put that matter to bed, you might as well have been raised by wolves."

The fact was that both he and Yusuf were sons of the same father. Yusuf's mother, a Muslim herself, had raised Yusuf out of wedlock as a Muslim, herself. Their father had denied paternity of Yusuf. The scandal forced Yusuf's mother to flee Germany and to return to Persia, to the ancient city of Iran, where Yusuf would be raised and educated. After Yusuf's father's death, a lawyer representing the estate informed Yusuf by letter that he had been willed a sizeable sum of monies and that his father's final wish was that Yusuf use the inheritance to journey to the New World and connect with his half-brother and start a new life. His half-brother, Ephraim Hirtz, who now went by Ephraim Hart, could be found in a city called *Philadelphia*. Hart had been contacted by the same attorney, and subsequently expected to hear from the Persian stranger. Yusuf made the arduous trek. They met for the first time on the corner of Market and Fourth in the city of brotherly love. It was now one score and three years later. They were very close allies businesswise.

Hart suffered a vertiginous inner sensation, in all probability caused by the thick coffee and cigar smoke which hung heavy in the Tontine Coffee House. The air could get so stiflingly thick in this place that it was common for men to just pass out cold.

"Permit me to speak on behalf of the Roman Catholic Church," arose a deep baritone voice from the hullabaloo. "Usury of all manner is forbidden." It was Jonny Bush. Freakishly silent he had been seated at the small round table adjacent to theirs. He was also a man of the Buttonwood Agreement, and so Hart was bound to him by covenant.

Bush had been listening to the two men. But given the clamor of the hundred or so gentlemen doing business in the small abode, and the insidious auctioneers out on the balcony calling to the crowd below, it would be surprising if he had heard much.

"If I recall correctly," he said, "Saint Thomas Aquinas in his superior work the *Summa Theologica* had argued that usury was immoral because it demanded recompense from a man *twice* for the sale of a single object—once for the object itself and once for the subsequent *use* of the object. The sin arises in such cases from the fact that the very nature of the object, Sirs, its very *essence*, is determined *by* its use, by its Aristotelian final cause if you will. Since the nature of the object, the *whatness* of the object itself, is identical to its *use*, one would be charging a man *twice* for one and the same thing. Usury would be a form of fraud. His example related it to a man's demanding from a second man payment for food sold to him, but then in addition, demanding extra payment for the food's subsequent ingestion. His point, I believe, Sirs, was that the *ingestion* of the food was the principal reason for the original purchase; the food was not being purchased for any other reason. Its ingestion was that for the sake of which the object was the object it was."

Bush stopped and stared at the cup in his hands and took a sip. He continued his train of thought.

"Turning to the lending and borrowing of money, then, the principal purpose of a man's borrowing money is to *spend* it once borrowed—not to simply keep it in his possession. To do so would render the money useless, and thus of no value to the borrower. In fact, in not being spendable it would no longer *be* money! As with food, its *use* defines its *essence*. Do you see? Borrow money and you borrow something to be *spent*. Spending it is the point of borrowing it. Usury arises when a man lends money to another and then demands repayment for the initial money lent and then *in addition* demands payment for the borrower's subsequent use of said money. Of course, it is possible, I suppose, that the additional demand is to compensate the original lender insofar as, in lending the money, he no longer possessed it, and so was denied the opportunity to spend it himself during the time of its having been borrowed. But in any event, the lender charges a man twice for a single object."

"You know a lot about usury," said Yusuf.

"I know a lot about sodomy, too!" Bush added. "Are you acquainted with the *I*-talian poet Dante? Both usurers and sodomites occupy the same ring of Hell. I shall repeat this with expatiation: the *same* ring of Hell, Sirs!" Bush again whiffed his thick black Turkish coffee, to which he added a heaping of sugar and spot of hot cream. Froth clung heavily to his outturned moustache.

"Blasphemers are there as well, I believe," Hart added.

"Aye, blasphemers," Yusuf said.

"So it is, I see, that we have all read our Dante. Impressed I am." Bush wiped the froth from his upper lip with the backside of his hand. "So, you know what sodomy is, I take it? Or must we endeavor to speak further of it in the Socratic manner, carefully defining our terms and the like? Speak now, I beseech you." Bush's eyes closed, his unibrow peaking at the center of his forehead. He groaned as he sipped his coffee, though barely detectable to the outer sense of audition.

Yusuf pondered Bush's proposal.

"Now, as I comprehend matters," Bush continued, "Mister Hart, thou wouldst appear to have the blessing of the Almighty to demand interest on money loaned so long as those from whom you demand interest are not of your religious persuasion."

"Correct," Hart replied. "But you, Sir, how is it that *you* escape the fires of Hell, I wonder, when you submit to the decrees of the Lateran Council and to the arguments of your Saint Thomas Aquinas? You are a banker, correct? Unlike myself, who is just a seller of stocks. So I take it that this sort of thing troubles you when lending money to Roman Catholics?"

"Me?" Bush mused. "Hell, I am no Catholic, Sir. I am an Episcopalian. Neither your ancient Mosaic laws nor the heathenesque rituals of the Holy Roman Catholic Empire apply to an Episcopalian. Push come to shove, Mister Hart, given that the Lord Jesus Christ died for my sins—past, present, *and* future, thank you very much—I am as much at liberty to commit usury as I am sodomy. All I have to do is ask our Lord and Savior to intercede for me and obtain our Holy Father's forgiveness, at which time all evil deeds performed prior to the act of asking are infinitely separated from my eternal soul distance-wise, as far as East is from West are they my sins separated from me." He produced a pack of chewing tobacco from his inside coat pocket, pinched off a rather large piece, and stuck it deep between his bottom gum and distal lip. "Usury and sodomy," he repeated entrancedly, "Oh...and blasphemy, can't forget blasphemy" he added, staring intensely all the while at the porcelain cup cradled in his tiny hands.

# 3

Hart retired early from the Tontine Coffee House. He exuded the redolent of roasted coffee beans and cigar smoke. His ears rang. It was late December and his wife, Frances, would be expecting him soon because it was Chanukah. Frances, his wife, was not Jewish, but Baptist. Even so, she had made it a point in their marriage to always recognize and honor holy days that appeared on the Hebrew calendar—specifically, given her interest in astronomy, those that fell on solstices and equinoxes.

The cold bit at his pale face as he made the walk home, the interiors of his nostrils and proximal tips of his ears getting the worst of it.

He walked up Wall Street past Federal Hall, the nation's capitol building for four years. George Washington and the new Congress had recently moved the federal government to Philadelphia, abandoning the Wall Street location. There was talk of a move further south. Washington was inaugurated on the second-floor balcony of Federal Hall. Hart looked at it and remembered the bitterly cold day. The city's government now occupied the building.

Hart reached Broadway. His abode was 74 Broadway, which was nearester the intersection of Broadway and Wall Street than any other building. The two-story building was a quasi-duplex. Three predicates each of the two households shared were a dividing wall, a grey slate roof, and a common portico. The interior of the portico was paneled with an unnamable brown wood. Between the two front doors sat the only red fustian velveteen love seat in the whole of the Lower East Side. Hart had sat on it maybe once.

His original surname was Hirz. He was born in 1747 in Franconia, Germany. He entered university at ten years of age, attending Julius-Maximilians-Universität Würzburg, which in its second founding in 1545 was fiercely Roman Catholic. In 1734 a new student charter had been established, so about twenty years before he would enter the university. The new charter would require the university to accept non-Catholic students, though it would take another two decades before it would accept Jews. Hirz was in fact the first, and possibly the last to attend.

He completed a Baccalaureate degree in 1765 in then his eighteenth year. He worked and saved for ten years following that and purchased passage to North America. He set out for the New World in March of 1775. Like most things in his history, the foregoing details of his education aside, it was the little things that prompted the largest changes in his life.

Here is how Hirz became Hart.

Passage from Franconia required that Hirz first make his way to the North Sea. After several days of delay, he boarded ship, the entire journey costing him seven pounds Sterling. The small ship sailed north and then west on the Rhine to Rotterdam, which took two weeks and one day. After a delay of three additional days in Rotterdam, he boarded yet another ship, this one much greater in size, which set out across the North Sea for Liverpool, England. There, the ship took in well over one hundred additional sojourners headed for America. But there were already over three hundred migrating souls onboard ship by the time it set out for England.

Much of the delay in Liverpool was caused by what appeared to be a large-scale military endeavor. The English seemed eager to pay a visit to their colonial brethren in the New World. The last of the warships had set sail two weeks earlier. Fortunately for Hirz and his four hundred fellow travelers the bulk of the military exercise had been undertaken over the preceding three months. He was witness to only the last of it.

The passage across the cold black Atlantic took twelve weeks. The malodorous ship finally ported in Philadelphia the eighth of June. Between 1727 and 1775 over one hundred thousand Germans had migrated through this port city. That was a lot of Germans; even according to Germans. But upon disembarking, his aspirations were laid into the ground, for the passengers were accosted by the dreadful news of war. It had been that during their journey across the great ocean those aforementioned warships had not arrived with gifts from English brethren, but England had in fact engaged militarily with the colonists, the engagements officiously titled in the papers "The Battles of Lexington and Concord."

Hirz could speak English, though not very well. His accent made his name sound to English ears as though he was saying *hurts*. He noticed that his fellow passengers almost always responded upon introductions with the query: "Hurts? Why, yes, leaving one's home will do that. But cheer up, young man, new adventures await you in the New World." As introductory rounds transpired over the next several weeks, fellow passengers referred to him as the man who likes to complain. Mrs. Charles Aberdeen had said within earshot to a woman with a child swaddled at her bosoms: "Enough already with telling us about his hurtings. He hurts. He hurts! Well, I'm hurting and you don't see me telling everyone. Do you see me telling everyone? I ask you, Sir, do you see it?"

"Sir?" replied the child-swaddled woman.

"My apologies," replied the great Mrs. Charles Aberdeen. "You look like a man."

"*Scheiss drauf!*," said Hirz, this after hearing the earshotted remarks, and thereafter introduced himself as "Hart". He further rationalized the change in name by reminding himself that he had embarked upon this journey as part of self-reinvention. Whether to keep or abandon his Jewish identity was never a point he considered. He would remain a Jew. But what better way to minimally reinvent oneself than to abandon the name given to him by the fates? Surely the *name* wasn't what conferred his Jewishness upon his humanly nature. The thing that mattered concerning his relation to the ancient tribe of

Judah, at least according to his mother, was what he had inherited from his mother. And quite clearly his surname was not this.

He nodded in the affirmative to officials as he passed through the tall iron gates of the port city of Philadelphia with a new nominal identity—*Ephraim Hart*.

# 4

Hart stood before his house and admired it. A long way from Franconia. The bells of Trinity Church rang out from across the street. It was still in the throes of being rebuilt. The church had been destroyed in a fire several years back. It was speculated that the fire had originated in the Fighting Cocks Tavern. If the *thing*—the church, I mean—could be taken as a metaphysical subject of change, as a *substance*, as Hart was prone to think of it, then *it* had simply undergone a material change, not unlike a living organism. Matter enters, stays awhile, and exits. The organism remains one and the same organism. Change requires that something remain *un*changed. Thus one would not be speaking of generation and corruption of a substance, but only of alteration. It was one and the same church that now disturbed the peace with its incessant bell-ringing as had disturbed the peace before the great fire.

It was pretty common for Hart to run into George Washington when walking Wall Street. But since the move to Philadelphia, Washington only made occasional visits. Hart had even once chatted with the great man.

The story goes something like this.

The newly appointed reverend of Trinity Church, Samuel Provoost, had consulted with legislators when ratifying the church's new charter, it having broken recently with England officially its ties. It needed to be shown that it was no longer loyal to its former boss, the King of England. For these legislators Hart had been working, and it was they who had set up the brief encounter with the great general.

Washington had asked Hart his thoughts on Adam Smith's *An Inquiry into the Nature and Causes of the Wealth of Nations*, published at the start of the War. Hart confessed that he had not read it but had it on his list of books to be read that year. About this Hart was lying. Few people Washington encountered had in fact ever heard of the book, let alone read it. One ass-kissing legislator for whom Hart worked claimed to have read parts of it. His critique of the book was that it was too big.

Hart had hoped originally that his encounter with Washington had marked a rise in his socio-economic status. He later learned that the motives of those legislators were not aimed at raising him with the strong grip of the lion's paw, as Freemasons would put it when speaking of bringing someone into their exclusive circle, but at showing how diverse and tolerant the new nation had become by introducing Washington to a successful "Americanized" German Jew. Hurting Hart's feelings had become impossible long ago. So, their motives were of no concern to him. That he had met the great man was the thing to remember.

Washington reported that neither he nor Alexander Hamilton had any affinity for Smith's book. Apparently, several of the nation's "founders" had formed a book club that met regularly during the War. Smith's book was on its reading list. Washington specifically did not think that the economic system devised by Smith would serve the ideals on which the new nation had been founded. Hamilton, however, quickly warmed up to it. Inspired by the book, at the very first session of the new Congress, he would propose the formation of the First Bank of the United States.

Hamilton was soon appointed Secretary of the new Treasury. He was not Washington's first choice. He really didn't like Hamilton all that much. Rather, Washington had first approached the great financier Robert Morris, who was known to have single-handedly arranged the bulk of the funding for the War. Morris had declined Washington's offer, however, and suggested that he approach Hamilton. Now in power, Hamilton wished to institute a national currency and a federal taxation scheme.

Concerning the capitalization of the bank, Hamilton would propose that it sell ten million dollars in stock, two million of which would be purchased immediately by the newly formed federal government. The remaining eight million would be made available to the public. Trouble was, the newly formed government did not have two million to spend. War had put the new nation into significant debt. What to do? Hamilton proposed that the federal government take out a loan from the soon-to-be First Bank of the United States and with that money purchase the stock.

An infamous "chicken-or-egg" debate loomed large among economic philosophers. The bank, in order to exist, required capital from investment, and yet for investors like the federal government to possess the money to invest, the bank had to loan the funds, and so for the scheme to work the bank would have to exist before it existed. Like many things economical, a bank's capital could be conjured out of thin air. Economical metaphysics went far beyond what Aristotle would have approved of, for it violated the Parmenidean principle: *Something cannot come from nothing*.

By some reports Hamilton would say, in light of the previous Bank of North America, that the First Bank of the United States was to be a *private* company. It would be a private company "owned" by the government and the public. Heads spun just trying to think the thought.

A question was posed on the floor of the new Congress about the details of the ten million. Would not the bank have to first raise this amount *before* it was allowed to loan it? *No*—was the reply. It simply needed to have on-hand at any given time five percent of the ten million. Thus, it could be the case that the bank possessed a mere five-hundred thousand dollars while being allowed to loan up to ten million. Unlike a human being, a bank need not have the money it loaned. Economical metaphysics 101.

Jefferson and Madison opposed the idea of a national bank, arguing that the amassing of financial power at the federal level threatened local and state financial institutions. Several laughed out loud at this and called the two *pussies*. A centralized bank, Jefferson and Madison continued, would only benefit big business interests in the north. Farmers of the south would be screwed. Hamilton stood firm, defending the One-Percentile—the biggest of the big business interests. Hamilton won the day. From the ranks of the One-percentile would come the priests of capitalism, the church of economical metaphysics.

The bells stopped ringing; time for Hart to get out of the cold.

# 5

"It smells good in here," Hart sang as he removed his overcoat in the narrow entryway. "I must be in the wrong house." He hesitated, and then added, "That was a joke, of course. I meant no offense, woman."

The boy Joel, Hart's son by marriage, poked his head out from the front room. He had recently turned nine. Frances, widowed almost eight years now, had met Hart through friends. She was Baptist. Joel had been claimed by the Baptists through the rite of baptism, and, to satisfy James' family after his death, as the only way to keep her son, she had promised to raise Joel a Baptist.

Frances made all this clear to Hart, who, in being a good man and in valuing promise keeping, had agreed to support Frances in continuing to raise the boy a Baptist—despite the fact that the few Baptists he knew seemed to be a bit off their theological rockers.

Even though she kept her promise to the Baptist church, the family, in acting in the fashion of a typical tolerant Christian family of the time, disowned Frances and the boy, exiled for the sin of Frances' having married a Jew. They insisted that a return to the family was possible only upon Hart's public conversion to the Baptist faith. Frances, who never really liked James' family, was secretly relieved that she would never have to see that lot again. Even so, she and Hart kept their promise, and the boy grew up a Baptist—well, sort of.

Neither Hart nor Frances had viewed their theological differences as an issue. Both were in need of companionship, both were loyal companions, and their marriage was based on trust and respect—not on the mechanically cold demands of theology.

Joel, as he would grow older, would give religion a thorough going-over, and would find himself closer in matters theological to a stubborn celebrity of the new nation, one Mr. Thomas Jefferson. As it would turn out, later in life, Joel would hear rumors about a *Bible* that Jefferson had fabricated, which reflected an interesting view some would call *Deism*. But Joel would question even that view as his rational faculty sharpened.

As time marched on, Joel would become a fan of *The System of Nature*, written by the French-German philosopher Paul-Henri Thiry, or as his friends freakishly called him, Baron d'Holbach. Since this work argued against Deism, and instead for a kind of atheism, Paul-Henry Thiry, or perhaps more accurately, Baron d'Holbach, wisely published the book under the name Jean-Baptiste de Mirabaud. Yeah, you heard that right. Two fake names removed from his own. Some say that this was done as a way of avoiding persecution by religious authorities—especially those tolerant Christian ones. And if anyone was good at persecuting, Christians were among the best. I'm serious—the best. As it would turn out, Joel would never know who had actually authored his favorite book. The two fake names removed thing had worked its magic. Be that as it may, it had a great influence on his thinking, and his view would ultimately be aligned with the atheists of his day.

"Old baboon, did you see crazy half-Uncle Yusuf today?" Joel asked with some excitement. The boy Joel had made it his business to insult Hart at every opportunity. Hart, in trying to be a good stepfather, initially did his best to ignore the boy. As time went on, however, he learned to play along, and even to insert a jibe or two of his own. This game went on only when they were alone together. No other human being knew of the insult-game played between them. It was an intimacy that would define their relationship.

Now, the boy Joel had met the Muslim Yusuf only twice and had greatly enjoyed both visits. Hart made it clear to Joel that Yusuf was only his half-brother and given that the boy shared absolutely no blood with Hart, the boy's natural relation to Yusuf was exponentially diluted. Joel nevertheless found joy in those parts of the explanation of the essential differences between his stepfather and half-uncle that involved tawdry details associated with mistresses and bastards. The title of "crazy" came from Frances, who had met Yusuf only once. The boy had adopted the title immediately, as a show of affection.

"Did I see your *Uncle* Yusuf today?" Hart corrected, the removal of "half" being a gesture of civility. The room smelled of freshly baked bread and roasted pheasant with rosemary and sweet onions. Both had been recently lingering within the iron framework of the large stone fireplace that dominated the north wall of the great room, which wasn't really all that great size-wise, but was the biggest room of the tiny domicile, and so it had become known as the great room.

The bread and pheasant now adorned the table. The great room was the center of the house. He saw that Frances had brought out the steel tub, in which their baths were to be taken. Kettles of water hung on iron rods located in the fireplace, just above the fire. Although there was no evidence that Frances ever bathed, Hart believed that Frances likely took her baths while he and Joel were making short adventures out to the privies in the rear yard, or perhaps while he was at work. It was a mystery. Upstairs were two rooms. One was the master bedroom, in which all three slept at night. The second was Hart's study.

Joel had papers on the floor of the great room neatly stacked into several piles. He was playing his second favorite game, which he had invented just that evening, called "Bucket Shop." His clients were several chess pieces, strategically placed in a semi-circle.

Hart had correctly surmised that the pieces were part of something concocted by the boy in play, in which they were having a meeting with the great trader, Master Joel Hart himself. Joel, who remember was only nine, had an uncanny grasp of the ins and outs of capitalism, which was now working its way into the mainstream.

"Board meeting?" Hart asked.

"No. I'm devising a new way to make profits," Joel said.

"Well, I should be interested in hearing this," Hart replied.

"Take a seat and observe," the boy said. A subject of fancy then arose suddenly among his phantasms. His eyes flickered. He seized the opportunity, asking, "O mongoloid, thou raises capital for companies so that they can grow, yes?"

Hart was struck by Joel's use of the word "capital." He had only first encountered the word, used in this context, in Arthur Young's recent book *Travels in France*. His colleague, Travis Handak of 55 Broad Street, had claimed that the word had been used twenty years earlier by Adam Smith, but Hart would not know whether this was true, since he had not read Smith's book. The encounter with Washington quickly flickered before his mind. He was skeptical as to whether Handak had read the monstrously large book. Handak had a drinking problem.

"Yes, I raise capital for companies by selling shares of their companies to others." Hart confirmed.

"What happens if a company fails? To the shareholders I mean, what happens to *them* if the company fails? Are they killed? Are they rendered slaves?" He stared with anticipation. "Hurry up with your reply already, my fancy can hold for only so long."

"Shareholders? You know that word too. My, my."

"Yes, I'm old beyond my years. I'm Oedipus in the making."

"Plotting my death and entertaining relations with your mother no doubt...," the bit about motherly relations mumbled under breath so that Joel could not make it out. He took a moment and then replied, "Nothing happens to them, you twit—"

"*Twit*—well done, Sir" the boy replied.

"Thank you," Hart replied. "Nothing happens to the shareholders mind you, as people I mean, but they do lose the money they invested."

Joel continued his interrogation. "A kind of *financial* death, then? Interesting. So, death *is* involved here, just not people death. Do *you* lose money?" Again, his stare intensifying. "My question, old man, get to the core of it—I beseech you on behalf of my fleeting phantasms."

"No. Once the trade is made, my work is done. Sheesh."

Frances could be heard walking overhead. Now down the stairs. She entered the room from the foyer. "I told you, Joel, put all of that away!"

"Yes, mother," Joel said.

Frances exited.

The boy adjusted the chess pieces.

"You have three minutes!" Frances shouted from the foyer.

"We have three minutes," Hart repeated. "I hope your phantasms can hold out. To get to the quick of it, I say that shareholders lose the money they invested if the company fails, but I do not lose a dime. And none of this involves *death*. What does all of this have to do with your game?"

"Well, remember when you took me to that bucket shop which does not in fact sell buckets?"

Hart looked back at the foyer. The coast was clear. "Now we made a deal you monkey child that we would never speak of that place when at home. Your mother does not approve of such places. That is a secret between us hairless baboons, or mongoloids, or whatever we happen to be this week."

"I never agreed to the deal, old man," Joel said.

"Is this the game you now play?" Hart asked.

"Yes, I call it *Bucket Shop*!"

"Son of a biscuit eater!" Hart loudly blurted out. He and Joel paused to see whether Frances would respond. Nothing.

"Remember the place?" Joel whispered back.

Hart composed himself, though his eyeballs bulged a bit.

"Of course, you dimwit. But a bucket shop is where *wagers* are placed against the rise and fall of stock prices, profits, what have you. These are not investments proper. Your mother shall indeed kill me when she discovers that I have introduced her precious boy to the sins of gambling."

"Yes, she will if she discovers, but she will never make the discovery," the boy whispered, mimicking Hart's bulging eyeballs.

"Your argument is invalid," Hart said with some urgency.

"Invalid, you say?"

"Yes. You claim that if she discovers, then she kills. You then assume that she does not discover. Clearly, you conclude that she does not kill. This is an instance of denying the antecedent, an invalid argument form. What am I paying your tutor for?"

"Very well, allow me to rephrase. She kills *only if* she discovers. There, I have made the discovery a necessary condition of the killing. Satisfied?"

"Yes, the logic is now impeccable. I feel safer just thinking about it." Hart said.

"How awesome is this our faculty of reason. I can manipulate reality itself with a simple rearrangement of propositions or logical operators," Joel said while gazing mysteriously into space.

"You are the Devil, you know that?" Hart said.

"I do, Sir, if by Devil you mean *Capitalist*!"

Frances entered the room wiping her hands with a white cotton dishtowel. "Alright Abraham and Isaac, your three minutes are up."

# 6

After their visit to Prune Street Prison, Hart and Joel began the long ride back to New York. They would have to again pass through the dark woods of the ass William Penn.

Joel was now a man. Fifteen. Had he been Jewish, Hart once remarked, he could have celebrated *bar mitzvah* at thirteen. That would have resulted in some serious cash, something that Joel found noteworthy. As it stood, the only rite of passage available to him as a nominal Baptist was to be almost drowned again.

"Let me get this straight," said Hart to Joel, who upon becoming a man had insisted on being called *The Capitalist*, "we make a profit by buying *high*? This is discombobulated! One buys low and *sells* high. Profits are made in this fashion."

"No, no, you imbecile," The Capitalist retorted, "you are not listening."

"O, I am listening alright," replied Hart.

"Let me construct the idea again and lay it bare before your meager mind." The Capitalist took a deep breath and sighed. "We do not *buy* anything—at least not at first. Do you not recall our discussion with my magnificent giant? His account of the canal company?"

"I recall our meeting with him, of course, I mean the man *is* a giant. You don't forget something like that. But for the life of me I cannot recall the details of his financial shenanigans. His massive head made it difficult for me to concentrate my humors." Hart paused for a second and then asked, "So, let me ask you a simple question: if we do not purchase the stock, how on earth do you plan on acquiring it?"

"As I was saying, the aim of what I call the *Wee* is to sell high and buy low."

"And you call it *Wee* why?"

"*Wee* refers to the aim of buying low. You know? Wee, meaning, short?"

"Dammit, man, you have the principle of investment all wrong," Hart insisted.

"No, I have it right!" retorted The Capitalist.

"Run it by me all the way through, and I'll make my judgment about its alignment with the principle of investment," Hart said.

"In order to perform the Wee, one first *obtains* stock A from broker Jones."

"Who's broker Jones? Do we know him?" asked Hart.

"He's just your run-of-the-mill general broker."

"General broker you say?"

"Seriously, this again? You and your obsession with the notions of *general* and *particular*."

"Let it go for now," granted Hart. "One purchases stock A from broker Jones. Then what?"

"No, you idiot. One does not *purchase* stock A; one *borrows* stock A—"

"Borrows?—"

"Recall the giant's account!"

"Goddammit, I don't recall the giant's account," Hart reminded.

"We convince Broker Jones to *lend* us stock A by proposing a financial deal that he cannot refuse. We promise to return stock A to him after an agreed upon period of time—say six months—and then as the sweetener we propose to pay him the price of the stock at the time of our returning it."

"What? Return the stock *and* pay him the going price after six months of maturity? We're not only left without stock, but we're out a handsome amount of money. Besides, *Wee* just calls to mind *Pee*. *That's* what you should call it." Hart felt a pressure in his chest.

"Not stupid," replied The Capitalist, "Why is your mind always in the gutter, man?"

"O, it *is* stupid because it's a lose-lose situation, and you should call it *Pee*. I don't need your permission. I'm just going to call it that." Hart exclaimed; the pressure in his chest increasing.

"Here, let me put some flesh on the bones of my plan before you explode," said The Capitalist. "Let the price of stock A at the time we borrow it be one dollar. Got it? We promise broker Jones that if he loans us stock A today, regardless of its going price, we will return stock A to him at the close of six months and pay him its going price at the six-month mark. Our promise is supposed to look a lot like we're promising to pay interest on the borrowed stock. He's thinking that not only will he get his stock back in six months, which he can then sell to someone else, and which he expects will be worth more than when he first lent it to us, but he will in addition be paid a higher price for stock A than he would have been paid had he sold it to us today. He'll see it as a win-win."

"Seriously, you don't hear how crazy that sounds? It is a win-win, for *him*." Hart said.

"Crazy only if the stock *rises* in value over the six months," replied The Capitalist. He paused, letting the idea sink in.

Hart's eyebrow stood erect revealing a sparking of the light of reason. Bingo!

"Continue," Hart said, head titled slightly, eyes looking upwards so as to acknowledge that the Promethean fire had in fact been lit.

"My plan exploits broker Jones's holding the expectation that the value of stock A will increase over the six-month period."

"And it is *not* going to increase, you're saying?" Hart asked.

"Correct. The idea runs thus. Suppose that over the six-month period instead of increasing, the value of stock A *decreases* considerably. Plummets even. Let's say that it falls to a low of a penny."

"A penny! And you're advocating our buying it? It cost us a dollar!" The fire almost flickering out.

"Think it through, old man. The plan is not to *keep* the borrowed stock. No. We sell it immediately upon our receiving it. For, the plan requires that on the day we borrow it, the day we sell it, the stock be at its *highest* price. We will do what needs to be done, then, to bring the price down, the further down the better. By month six we want the price of that stock to be at its rock bottom."

"Oh, I see, soon after we borrow the stock, we sell it to someone and no longer possess it. We now have a dollar. I'm with you this far." The Promethean embers began to crackle and hiss, promising to reignite.

"Correct. So, as I said earlier, let's say that at the time we borrow it, stock A is priced at a dollar a share. Broker Jones lends it to us. We immediately turn and sell it at its current price of a dollar."

"Yes, but I take it that we'll be buying more than a single share," Hart clarified.

"Yes, of course," The Capitalist confirmed. "But keep the math simple for now. So, we no longer own stock A but have a dollar. As I said, we do stuff during the six-month interim that will make the price of stock A plummet, where at the close of this six-month period it is valued at a penny." The Capitalist paused, and then continued, "At month six we then go to some other broker, call him broker Smith—"

"And broker Smith is also a general broker?" interrupted Hart.

"Yes, he's a general broker, though I'm not sure why that is relevant," answered The Capitalist.

"How is he distinct from broker Jones?" asked Hart.

"Distinct?"

"Yes, how does one tell broker Jones apart from broker Smith, if both are *general* brokers?" asked Hart, "Wouldn't they, in being general, be indiscernible? For, I take it that by *general* here you mean something like *abstract*?"

"I can't believe that you're going to make us discuss this again."

"Believe it, don't believe it—but I see no way around it."

"Fine. Run by me your silly philosophical concern over our referring to brokers Jones and Smith as *general* brokers," The Capitalist invited.

"Not so silly, as you'll no doubt see in what's coming. Now, the great English philosopher John Locke worked out what we mean when talking about general or abstract things, like the general idea of a triangle. Do you want to hear what Locke said?"

"Do I have a choice?"

"Locke begins his analysis with the idea of a particular triangle, such as the idea of a three-four-five right triangle."

"A three-four-five right triangle?"

"Yes, a right triangle whose sides measure three, four, and five units respectively. The side measuring five units is the hypotenuse."

"Okay, a three-four-five triangle. Got it."

"If we now remove from the idea—"

"Wait, what do you mean by *idea*?"

"Locke says that an idea is whatever it is that one thinks about when thinking."

"That doesn't help," said The Capitalist.

"Think about a triangle."

"Does it have to be a three-four-five right triangle?"

"No, think of any old triangle."

"Okay, I'm thinking of one," said The Capitalist.

"That, my young princess, is your *idea* of a triangle."

"Are you saying that I'm thinking about my *idea* of a triangle, or about a *triangle*?"

"Come again?" asked Hart.

"Is the thing before my mind an *idea* of a triangle or a *triangle*?"

"Well, I suppose that they are one and the same."

"Suppose I think of a chicken pie," said The Capitalist.

"Okay, I was hoping to stick to triangles, but go on..."

"I'm thinking of a chicken pie. Is the thing before my mind the *idea* of a chicken pie, or it is a *chicken pie*?"

"Well, since the chicken pie is what you're thinking about, I suppose that the thing before your mind would be a chicken pie," Hart replied.

"But if it *were* a chicken pie," said The Capitalist, "I'd be able to eat it. Right?"

"Okay, so maybe we need to say that it is your *idea* of a chicken pie," replied Hart.

"But if the idea of a chicken pie is what is before my mind, and what is *not* before my mind is a chicken pie, we must deny that they are one and the same thing—the *idea* of the pie and the *pie*."

"Yes. What's your point?" asked Hart.

"My point, you dimwit, is that as in the chicken pie case, my idea of the triangle and the triangle itself cannot be said to be one and the same thing."

"Go on..." Hart mused.

"Go on? The point is made!"

Hart looked confused.

"So, which is before my mind when I think about a triangle," demanded The Capitalist, "an *idea* of a triangle or a *triangle*?"

"I'd like to say that they are one and the same thing."

"I know that that is what you'd *like* to say, but *can* you say it?"

"Why are we talking about this?" asked Hart.

The Capitalist gave Hart a most stern stare.

"Can I finish telling you about my plan?" asked The Capitalist.

"After we eat. I'm starving," Hart said. "I'm thinking chicken pie."

# 7

The boys came across a Dutch Amish tavern just outside of Philadelphia that was serving chicken pie. Serendipitous. It was indeed a spectacle to see the advanced state of the Amish. They and the larger surrounding German communities had become so advanced and economically abundant that at one point in the new nation's rise it was hotly debated as to which language the government would use in the expressing of its laws: German or English. For some reason Dutch wasn't in the race. Hart had agreed with an Amish patron of the tavern that they were living in the most modern of times. The enlightenment was here. The Amish would no doubt continue living on the cutting-edge of things—especially with respect to ingenuity and technology. Times surely could not ever get much more advanced than this. The Capitalist disagreed strongly with both men.

After lunch they mounted their horses and returned to the long ride back to New York, which, it should again be mentioned, would take them through the dark woods of the ass Mister Penn.

"Good chicken," said Hart.

"Man, this is getting old," The Capitalist said while taking a moment to shake his limbs as though waking himself from a heavy sleep. "So, let's get back to it. Now, I was saying, once we have borrowed stock A from broker Jones, and have sold it for a dollar—"

"Wait, I remember what I wanted to talk about—*general* brokers," Hart declared with widened eyes.

"I gave you your opportunity to blab about general brokers over lunch."

The Capitalist looked away and sang a short verse from his favorite song, something he had to do sometimes when talking with Hart.

"Like I was saying," continued The Capitalist, "at month six we find a new broker, broker Smith—goddammit, don't say it—and from broker Smith we buy stock A for a penny, its going price. We then go back to broker Jones and return to him stock A, as promised, and pay him stock A's value at the close of this period, the close of month six, which, as our current thought experiment predicts, is a penny."

"So, we began month one with a dollar after selling stock A," Hart summarized, "and at the close of month six, after purchasing stock A from broker Smith for a penny, returning the newly purchased stock A to broker Jones as promised, while also paying broker Jones the price of stock A, which is now only a penny, we have paid out only two cents, leaving us with a balance of ninety-eights cents profit."

"Yes! Do you see? We made ninety-eight cents without ever investing a single penny! Multiply this by thousands of shares, and we will make a fortune."

"Hey, I just thought of another application of your word *Wee*," said Hart. "*Wee* can refer to the short interval of time between our getting stock A and our selling it. We could say that we're 'short-selling,' or maybe 'short-holding'—in any event short something. We don't have to use *Wee*. It's kind of weird." He paused and then continued, "But, what's been bothering me is that part of your plan that requires us to do 'stuff,' as you mysteriously call it, in order to make the value of stock A plummet. What sort of 'stuff' do you have in mind? Like I said, we can do this only if it is on the up and up."

"You and that up and up. What the hell does that mean? Up and up. But I agree, that is the real challenge of the plan. I still need to work that part out." The Capitalist thought for a moment, then added, "But, I like the way that stupid Johnny managed the collapse of my glorious giant's canal company. We might adopt something like that for our plan."

"You and that giant should just get a room and be done with it," Hart said.

"If only such were possible," mused The Capitalist.

"Stupid Johnny?" Hart lit up, "I recall him from our blabbing with the giant. So, his enormous head didn't erase *everything* after all. I recall...what was his name?...was it Stretch?"

"*Stench*, I think," The Capitalist answered.

"Yes, Stench. Strange name that," Hart confirmed. "It occurs to me that in borrowing and then in selling the stock as is called for by your Weeing that there is no investing going on. We are only pretending to help finance the company that is offering stock A. In fact, we are hoping for its *demise*. No?"

"Yes," said The Capitalist, "we are not investing in the company, and we are betting that it fails."

"But doesn't that belie the very aim of investment?" Hart asked.

"Who says that the purchase of stock is coextensive with investment?" The Capitalist asked back.

"Well, everyone, I figure."

"Naïve you are. Besides, I don't know about you, but I could care less about the success of another's business," The Capitalist added. "Show me where it says that when one purchases stock that one is aiming to *support* the success of a company. Show me! Not even your stupid Buttonwood Agreement states such a thing."

"I admit that it's not really written anywhere. I just assumed that that was the point of our financial system," Hart said. "But let's say for sake of argument that when purchasing stock one isn't necessarily hoping for the success of the company whose stock it is. Betting against a company's success does reek of the nefarious sort of thing obsessed gamblers hope for when at Bucket Shops and whatnot. So, this sort of thing isn't new, I guess." Hart took a second to think and then asked, "So, if it's not written anywhere, I take it that this Weeing or Shorting, or whatever we call it, is *legal*?"

"Probably," said The Capitalist.

"Probably? Is it *moral* then?" asked Hart.

"Moral? What matters this?" asked The Capitalist.

"It matters quite a bit, I must now assert, and even more so to those who have read the books authored by my kinsman, the Great Honorable Herr Doctor Professor Immanuel Kant."

"Kant, you say? I thought that you were pushing Locke these days," said The Capitalist.

"Immanuel Kant, the great *German* philosopher," Hart said.

"I see that you shudder when speaking his name."

"You bet I do."

"What gives?" asked The Capitalist.

"Here's what gives. In his newest tome, *The Critique of Practical Reason*, Professor Kant introduces his handsome Categorical Imperative, which sets the standard for determining *moral* action. It states that it is immoral to do some action A if by willing the doing of A as a universal maxim one renders the willing of the doing of A impossible. Morals must be willable insofar as they are doable. Thus, if an action is not willable, it is not a moral action."

"The willing of the doing of *A*? Must we use *A*, since I have accustomed myself to thinking of A and A-like things in terms of my previous example of the Wee, where *A* denotes a stock. Can we recast your action A as action *B*?" The Capitalist pleaded.

"I suppose. But you miss the point. The idea is that—"

"I see the point."

"I do not think that you see it," Hart retorted.

"Oh, I see it alright. Let me expound my understanding of your fancy Doctor Kant," said The Capitalist.

"Hit it."

"Suppose that one contemplates the doing of B, as a moral act, I mean. According to your man Kant, they should ask: *Can* I *do* B?"

"Well, let me stop you right there, for it is a matter of *willing* to do B, not simply the *doing* of B."

"Fine. One asks, *Can I will to do B?* where the motivation for even asking the question is to determine whether action B is morally permissible. Better?"

"Yes, better. Proceed."

"The answer to this question is got *via* a thought experiment of sorts. One imagines that one has willed the doing of B to be a universal rule, a maxim, where all agents in situations of the kind in question are commanded to do B. If in willing this, in willing it to be *universal*, and the doing, excuse me, the *willing* of B is subsequently rendered impossible, then one should not do B, at least not within the context of considering possible *moral* actions, since the result of the thought experiment has shown that action B cannot be universalized. Hence, it is shown to lie outside the realm of possible moral actions."

"Yes, this sounds eerily correct. Weird that I am learning more from you than from the great doctor's book," Hart admitted. "Go on, please provide an example."

"An example," The Capitalist said as he put his forefinger to his lower lip and looked upwards, directing his animal spirits to stir in that direction. "Suppose that Williams asks Smith about the profit Smith..."

"Is this Smith our broker Smith?" asked Hart.

"No, no. It's another Smith."

"How are they distinct?" asked Hart.

"By the gods, man! Stick to the topic of Weeing."

"Okay."

"Where was I? Yes—Williams and Smith, who are partners, and..." The Capitalist said as Hart's face again lit up, "...By Zeus, don't say it..."

"Say what?"

"You were about to again ask whether partner Smith is broker Smith..."

"No, I wasn't."

"Sure looked like it. Now, Williams and—let's make Smith *Jefferson*; so, the partners are Williams and Jefferson. Got it? So,

Williams asks Jefferson what they had earned by way of the sale of stock jointly owned. Jefferson sold the stock at a profit of twenty dollars but wishes to lie to Williams, telling him that the profit was only ten. This way, Jefferson would only have to split the reported profit of ten dollars with Williams. Jefferson, in keeping the other ten secret, would pocket it along with the five he made post-split with Williams."

"This case of Williams and Jefferson sounds familiar. What profit did we earn upon the sale of our recent stock?" asked Hart, "Am I about to learn—"

"This is an *example*, you moron, not a confession," The Capitalist assured, while crossing his fingers behind his back. "Back to our example—Jefferson is a Kantian and asks himself, within a moral context, whether he can *lie* to Williams—or, perhaps it is that he wonders whether he can even *will* to lie to Williams. The thought experiment proceeds thusly. Jefferson imagines his willing it to be a universal maxim that in all such cases anyone asked for such information *must* lie."

"I'm following you thus far," said Hart.

"Good. So, suppose, then, that when asked about such a thing, like how much profit was made in the sale of the jointly owned stock, the maxim dictates that the one partner must lie to the other."

"Both know of the requirement to lie, the maxim?" asked Hart.

"Of course. It is a universal maxim. Both know of it."

"So, in such a case, Williams will *know* that Jefferson is lying?"

"Yes, exactly. And were the shoe on the other foot, Williams would be required to lie to Jefferson," added The Capitalist Joel.

"And Jefferson would *know* this?"

"Yes."

"But if everyone knows that in such cases the one partner must lie to the other, the lie cannot succeed, lying would no longer be *doable*. I mean, the point of lying is to deceive, and in the case that you've invented here, no partner could ever deceive the other. Lying has been rendered impossible in such situations," Hart reasoned.

"Yes," The Capitalist affirmed. "By willing lying to be a universal maxim in such cases the very *point* or *purpose* of lying has been rendered unachievable."

"And so, in cases like this, Jefferson *cannot* lie? It is as though it has become conceptually impossible to lie."

"Well, he *can* lie to Williams. The thought experiment has done nothing to the action itself. It's just that he could no longer lie if lying in such cases had been universalized. For, only universalizable actions are candidates for *moral* action. According to your Doctor Kant, then, because of this Williams should not lie, if what he's after is determining what is moral." answered The Capitalist.

"He cannot...*because*...?"

"Are you serious, old man? Were he to will it to be a universal maxim, he would in fact make it such that lying would no longer be an achievable action. And, by rendering it unachievable, it is shown to be an action that cannot be willed! Thus, lying in such cases is not among the possible moral actions. You were the one who first brought up your divine doctor. Do you not know his philosophy?"

"I thought I understood this stuff," Hart assured. "But now I'm not certain about my earlier certainty. If action B is an *immoral* act, it is one precisely because were one to will the doing of B to be a *universal* maxim, one would in fact make it such that one could not will the doing of B. There is a peculiar contradictory aspect to it. Since all moral actions are universal by their very nature, then if requiring an action to be universally performable rendered the action impossible, then such an action is by its very nature not a *moral* one. But now it would appear that Kant's impressive Categorical Imperative doesn't tell us so much which actions are moral, but instead only tells us which ones are not."

"Whatever. He's your guy."

"So, Kant is right on this one! Yes?" asked Hart.

"Well, *no*, for your beastly Kant is just wrong."

"Beastly?" asked Hart.

"Grotesque! Did you not see the engraving of your divine doctor's portrait included on a preface-page included in your book?" The Capitalist asked.

"You saw the book?"

"Yes, and I read it too!"

"You read the book?" asked Hart.

"Of course. How else would you explain my salient understanding of his faulty doctrines?"

"It would be difficult to explain, I grant you."

"You should steer clear of such a man. He looks like a pot-bellied pig on which someone has cleverly put a wig," said The Capitalist.

"Actually, now that you mention it," said Hart.

"This is reason enough to reject his philosophy!" declared The Capitalist.

"You appear to be right enough. Besides, I am a Utilitarian, and prefer calculating my actions based upon the amount of pleasure my actions will most assuredly usher into the world," Hart confessed.

"Now you are talking," said The Capitalist, "maximizing pleasure is the thing."

"And this that you propose to do—to Wee—is something that will maximize *our* pleasure, but won't it bring some pain to our broker Jones?"

"To be sure. And it will bring some pain to those poor saps who invested in stock A," added The Capitalist.

"To be sure," echoed Hart. "Do you think that the quantity of pleasure that you and I will acquire will outweigh the quantity of pain acquired by our broker and those saps you mention?"

"I think that it will most assuredly outweigh their pain," replied The Capitalist. "Of *that* I am sure."

"Of our pleasure outweighing their pain?"

"No, I am sure of how assuredly I think that it will," said The Capitalist.

"Until I better understand what you just said, that is good enough for me," said Hart.

They rode silently side by side for a while. Then Hart expressed a concern.

"So, tell me O great one," Hart sighed, "whether one can will it a universal maxim that one Wees."

"We are back to that again?" The Capitalist moaned.

"Yes. I was just thinking out my willing Weeing to be a universal maxim, and noticed that if everyone Wee'd, Weeing, or rather the willing to Wee, would be rendered impossible. Weeing cannot work if everyone Wees. And thus, the light of reason has revealed to me that I cannot will Weeing if I will it to be a universal maxim. Thus, Weeing would *not* be among the possible moral actions."

"So what!" The Capitalist retorted, "Lots of actions are like that. Actions we do every day."

"Like what?" Hart challenged.

"Well, there are plenty of actions that one can universalize and yet we would not call them moral actions. Like multiply and dividing."

"Multiplying and dividing?"

"We universalize the rules, the procedures, for multiplying and dividing, and by doing that we never render these rules impossible to follow. Right? And yet, no one thinks that multiplying and dividing are *moral* actions."

"Speak for yourself," said Hart.

"My point is that not all *universalizable* actions are moral actions," said The Capitalist. "Rather, the idea is that all moral actions are universalizable."

"I sort of get that," Hart admitted.

"It's like saying that not all mammals are cats. All cats are mammals, but not all mammals are cats."

"I get that. So, okay, then," replied Hart, "give me your best argument against Kant's view. But stay clear of the medieval categorical logic."

"Porcine creature with a wig—that is all I will say to you," replied The Capitalist.

"Okay, you got me there," said Hart as though having tasted something sour.

"Indeed. You make *me* shudder just thinking of his image." The Capitalist wiggled a little in his saddle, demonstrating his internal shudderings. "Why do you do this when you know full well that we shall be spending at least one night in this dark forest? Penn's Woods indeed! Your Doctor Kant will haunt me the entire night, no doubt, lurking behind these tall black trees, such phenomena underwritten only by the forms of intuition. *Can* there even *be* a thing in itself? A thing existing independently of the conditions of space and time, I mean? What are these trees *like* independently of the forms of intuition which I impose? Blankness is all I get here—not even *extended* blankness, mind you, for that presupposes space. I again shudder just thinking about the impossibility of thinking about it. There, you now have me at two shudderings—who is the asstard now!"

"Sounds like you peeked at my copy of the *Critique of Pure Reason*, too," Hart said, "I thought that it was well-hidden in my bureau."

"I did more than just peek at it. I perused it! And the work molested me. I hope that you are satisfied with yourself for bringing such Neoplatonist pornography into our home," said The Capitalist. "Seriously, man, I'm only fifteen."

"I shall no longer appeal to that hideous wigged pig man," said Hart, "but will again return to my Utilitarian musings."

"Good," said The Capitalist. "We shall both sleep better with the handsome image of Jeremy Bentham before our minds. Surely his superior head will always be firmly attached to his body."

"Not if his body were to be stuffed, say, the head severed, put under a bell jar or some such," Hart replied as though in a trance. "I am imagining it now. The head falling off its pedestal from time to time..."

The phantasm abused The Capitalist. "In Grimm's name, man, what is it with you and your gruesome sayings?"

"The gruesome is not in the world but in your *mind*," Hart replied in a creepy monotone voice.

"So now we're Bishop Berkeley, are we?" chided The Capitalist. You had better hope that I don't find a large stick sitting at the ready at our future campsite. I will beat you silly with it while you sleep."

Hart smiled at the thought of the toddler-man wearing himself out at trying to swing the large stick.

"Note to self," Hart said aloud, "stay clear of large-sticked areas."

"Note to self," retorted The Capitalist, "beat this Kantian senseless."

"Note to self," retorted Hart.

Silence.

"Well?" blurted The Capitalist.

"Well what?"

"Aren't you going to make the note to thyself?"

"What note?"

"I swear, old man, consider your brains smashed."

"No, *you* consider it, for the brains of which you smash are but an idea," retorted Hart mockingly philosophical.

# 8

Having taken a few days to recover from their return from Prune Street Prison in Philadelphia, Hart and The Capitalist dropped in on Mr. Carmichael. Carmichael was among several stockjobbers in New York authorized to sell stock in the recently formed First Bank of the United States. But Hart and The Capitalist were not interested in purchasing stock in the bank.

Payton Bell, a regular at the Tontine Coffee House, went to work for a company that relocated him somewhere up near the Mohawk River. He had recently returned with complaints about the deteriorating state of the company. He left before things grew too ugly. It was teetering on collapse. Hart was struck with glee to discover that this very same company was in the throes of recapitalization, looking for investors to purchase recently released company stock. It was The Western Inland Lock Navigation Company.

The company constructed lock-systems up and down canals, which made navigating upriver possible. The Western Inland Lock Navigation Company was set to build a system of locks along or near the Mohawk. This would secure shipping up and down the river. A very big venture.

Now, Hart and The Capitalist expressed to Carmichael great interest in this stock. And, as they expected, Carmichael praised it to no end. The stock had been increasing in value almost daily, to the tune of about seventy-five cents a week per issue of stock. Today's price for the stock was three dollars and twenty-seven cents.

Hart and The Capitalist set their scheme into motion—the one discussed on their ride back to New York: the Wee. They began by feigning that they had no available funds to purchase any stock today, having sunk all of their moneys into George Washington's Potomac Company, a company similar in kind to the Western Inland Lock Navigation Company. Washington's company had recently constructed a lock system along the Potomac. Their story gave the impression that they were really into construction of lock-systems.

About their investment into Washington's company, Hart and The Capitalist were fibbing, since Washington's company had never taken on investors. In fact, Washington had resigned as the company's president almost ten years earlier, just before becoming President of the United States in 1789. But Carmichael did not know this, knowing little of recent historical affairs. O how the two prayed for Carmichael's seeing a way of parting with the stock without their having to pay for it.

"In six months our dividends of the Potomac Company stock will come due," whispered The Capitalist to Hart, though loud enough for Carmichael to overhear. "Perhaps then we can purchase these stocks of The Western Inland Lock Navigation Company."

"Yes, this is how it will have to be," replied Hart. "But just think of it. If we *could* purchase these stocks today, imagine what they would be worth in six months!"

"Suppose," The Capitalist entertained, "that the stock increases in value along its current trajectory. Were we to purchase this stock in six months, we probably would not be able to afford it. But who knows? Our Potomac stock will surely increase over that time." Joel turned to Carmichael. "Sir, do you expect the stock's trajectory to be as we project, at a dollar or so a week per issue?"

"Why yes, your projection is highly probable, given the stock's history, though I would put the increase a bit lower, in line with how it has increased these past few weeks, at about seventy-five cents." asserted Carmichael clearly making the attempt to appear earnest as brokers go. He was finding the exchange about such a matter with such a young thing dressed in boy's clothes quite exciting. She was striking he thought, though too young for him to venture entertaining any further thoughts that the Lord might judge to be impure.

"The following has just come to me," said Hart. "Suppose, Mister Carmichael, and I'm just spit-balling it here, but suppose you were to *loan* us the stocks today, where we would take possession of them *today*, as I said and am now saying, *loaning* them to us *today*, and in six months we would return those stocks to you in full *and* pay you for them at the amount that they were worth at that time—at the close of month six, I mean. Would you be up for that?"

Hart's heart raced. He couldn't believe that he had made the move this early in the exchange.

"Let me be clear about this," said Carmichael. "I loan to you stocks today and you return them to me in six months along with a payment for those very stocks, the ones returned to me, where the amount you will pay me shall be the price at which they are valued at *that* time, six months from today?"

"Correcto munduo," replied Hart.

"I see what you are up to," interjected The Capitalist. "We are basically offering this good gentleman a type of bank security."

"Bank security?" asked Carmichael.

"It is an investment with the promise that at the end of some agreed upon period, both the principal invested, and interest gained will be returned," answered The Capitalist confidently.

"Okay," Hart interrupted, "maybe I am offering that?—but in any case I can affirm that the very possession of such a quality stock today would significantly increase the value of our portfolio, which would give us some extra umph to our future buying power. I do not know about you, my young partner, but I would surely feel superior in my possessing such a high-quality stock." Hart then turned to Carmichael. "But the financial benefit to us, Mister Carmichael, as I have been saying with emphasis, would be that the possession of these stocks would increase the value of our portfolio, a value that would allow us to make certain trades down the road and to secure certain loans perhaps as soon as tomorrow, without in fact having to sell what we currently own in stock for cash."

"Yes,...well no, but yes,...I can see the value in possessing them portfolio-wise. But your doings in the interim, your feelings of superiority, the acquiring of other loans, are of no concern to me. Use your portfolio any way you wish. Our accord is simply my *lending* you these stocks for six months, as a means of temporarily fancifying your portfolio, if I have what you just said correct, where at the close of this period of six months you will return them to me, this very stock, paying me the price they are worth at that time."

"Yup," said Hart.

"Although unconventional, I see nothing illegal or immoral in this," Carmichael said.

"You must be a Utilitarian," Hart said.

"A Unitarian?" Carmichael asked.

"Unitarian you say?"

"Yes, Unitarian," answered Carmichael.

"Perhaps this is a case of opaque reference," Hart replied.

"Opaque reference?" asked Carmichael.

"Pardon my business partner," interrupted The Capitalist, "he has read too many philosophical books. You should hear him on the road."

"Oh yes, philosophical. I see," said Carmichael.

Hart could see that Carmichael was still on the fence. He needed to give him a nudge.

"Of course, I understand that you may not wish to do this," said Hart, "to loan us the stock, I mean, in which case my partner and I will speak to the other good Mister Carmichael, your identical twin, who is also issuing stocks for The Western Inland Lock Navigation Company. People have told me that he would be very interested in a deal like this."

It was widely known that the Carmichael twins hated each other.

"Well—," Carmichael said, "who am I to deny anyone the feeling of superiority?"

An accord was struck official. Seeing the potential windfall, Carmichael took the upper hand and *insisted* on lending, as he took care to put it, two thousand shares, each currently valued at three dollars and twenty-seven cents, the total coming to six thousand, five hundred and forty dollars in stock.

The stocks were to be returned to him in six months, at which time Hart and his lovely young lady friend would pay him what the stock was worth as set at the close of six months. Carmichael computed the probable return: If a single stock rose just fifty cents a week, then at the end of month six, twenty-six weeks, it would be worth sixteen dollars and twenty-seven cents a share, or in all, thirty-two thousand, five hundred and forty dollars! He *also* would be getting all of the stock back that he had originally lent, which he could then sell for another thirty-two thousand, five hundred and forty dollars. Altogether, in only six months' time, he could turn a sixty-five hundred dollar "loan" into a sixty-five-thousand-dollar profit! He ran the scenario again through his thick mind. The mathematics of it was a real humdinger pleasure-wise. The image of kicking his brother in the nuts immediately accompanied the computation. Had Carmichael knew anything about Utilitarianism, he would have agreed with Bentham that intellectual pleasures were immensely greater than sensible ones.

"See you in six months," said Carmichael sternly, having completed the paperwork, being careful to mask the great joy that now stirred his animal spirits.

Once at a safe distance from Carmichael, The Capitalist said to Hart, "The first step of our plan is complete. We now must turn to selling these stocks at today's price and pocket the six grand. After that, we must turn our attention to the ruin of The Western Inland Lock Navigation Company."

"So mode it be," replied Hart sternly, in Masonic fashion, being careful to mask the great joy that now stirred his animal spirits.

# 9

Days before their encounter with the stockjobber Mr. Carmichael, Hart and the Capitalist had sojourned to Prune Street Prison, located in Philadelphia. The journey required two days ride from New York. Their hope initially was to find the great financier Robert Morris, who had recently taken up residence at the prison, a debtor's prison for those who could not pay their debts. The Capitalist knew that the great financier knew something, for one doesn't get into that much trouble without knowing *something*. It was the Capitalist's aim to know what that something was.

As the two set out on horseback, the sun hung high in its zenith. Sharply underneath all visible objects were cut the darkest shadows of the day. Their horses walked lazily over their own shadows, finding noticeable relief only when walking under the large elms. But other trees had slowly begun to push through the thick wall of giants—black and white walnut, cypress, pine, and cedar. The summer buzzing of the cicadas swelled and swooned. Birds lounged in the trees, some hopping to and froe on the ground as if playing a game of tag. Many sang, but interestingly none of those were ever visible. Hart could smell the earthy deep cold of the Raritan River as they made their approach to the bridge that would allow them to cross over.

After a restless night in Penn's Woods they arrived at Prune Street Debtors Prison, a bit after one o'clock Philadelphia time. The prison was, not surprisingly, located on Prune Street, between Fifth and Sixth, just south of another prison, the Walnut Street Prison, which was located on Walnut Street. Philadelphia was home to a lot of prisons.

The prison was a rather drab building, rectangular lengthwise, running east to west, lined with uniformed rows of small rectangular windows. Neither glass nor bars inhabited any of the window holes. If a man were thin enough, he could easily pass through his cell window and disappear into the night. But escape wasn't an issue, really, since incarceration was secured by the honor system.

The building lay open like an Italian monastery. At the center of its rectangularity stood a tallish bell tower minus the bell. Hart thought about the church across the street from his house. It smelled more like a stable than a place inhabited by human beings, but it wasn't foul. More "earthy" than anything. A substantial vegetable garden flanked the southeast side of the prison. Several men were working the garden, but like monks sworn to silence none spoke. The sun again appeared in its zenith, high up though this time ever so slightly to the north. Black shadows were cast almost directly beneath the objects that served as their originals, though reaching ever so slightly south.

"How do you suggest we find Mister Morris?" Hart asked.

"Why not just ask the guard there, the one nearest the door? He can surely direct our next steps," replied The Capitalist.

They dismounted, tied off their horses, and approached the guard.

"May I help you?" asked the impressively uniformed turnkey.

"Yes, we are here to see Mister Robert Morris," said Hart.

"Robert Morris, you say? Well, he's poplar these days."

"Poplar?" Hart probed. The annexed idea appeared—it was the idea of a tree, the very idea, in fact, that Hart *sometimes* employed when thinking the *abstract* tree. He had learned that this was what he did when thinking of abstract objects from his having read the readings of the famous Bishop Berkeley. Locke's treatment of such ideas had only gotten him into trouble philosophical-wise with The Capitalist. Hart would use his idea of the poplar to represent all ideas he had of trees. How often he wondered how he could tell whether the idea of this poplar he had used on Monday was the same that he had used on Tuesday. He—

"Sorry—pop-*u*-lar," said the turnkey. "I know how you Americans like your vowels."

"Yes, pop*u*lar," repeated Hart.

"Not three days ago President George Washington himself was here," said the turnkey.

"President Washington? He visited our Mister Morris?" asked Hart.

"Indeed. Spent the entire afternoon with him, he did."

"My, that *is* exciting," said The Capitalist.

"You are right, lil' missus," replied the turnkey. Then violently he shouted back into the black mouth of the prison—"Capt'n, Sir, we have visitors!"

From the dark hole they could hear heavy booted footsteps, increasing in volume as they drew nearer the light. A man not much taller than Joel emerged.

"Visitors, you say?" he called out.

"Yes, Sir, visitors for our Mister Morris."

"Visitors for our Mister Morris, you say?"

"Yes, Sir...for our Mister Morris."

"Mister Morris." The short and stout uniformed man looked squintingly at both Hart and The Capitalist. "Mister Morris, you say? Well, if that doesn't say it all. We just hosted a former President of these United States. Did you tell them, Will'ms, that the former President General George Washington was here, visiting our Mister Morris?"

"Yes, Sir. Not three days ago, I says to these two."

"Well if that doesn't say it all," repeated the captain. "I am Captain Johnson." He looked to Hart, "And you are...?" he said approaching with his right hand extended.

Hart immediately feared that if he didn't take hold of the extended appendage that it would surely make physical contact with the crotchal region.

"Ephraim Hart," replied Hart. He took Captain Johnson's hand, manipulating it in an upward direction, and shook it good and hard.

"And this sweet thing is..."

"O, this is Joel Hart, Sir," said Hart.

"Strange name for such a princess, but there you are, children these days with their disconventional denominations and such," said Captain Johnson.

"I am not a *princess*," assured The Capitalist.

"Take off your hat, then, and let's have a look at you," said Captain Johnson.

Joel removed his hat. Long blonde curls unfurled and fell to about his shoulders. The captain leaned forward.

"If that doesn't say it all then," blurted Captain Johnson. "Do you see this, Will'ms?"

"Mister Morris?" Hart reminded.

The captain leaned back but continued to inspect Joel. "Yes,...Mister Morris. We'll see to that." The captain leaned in again, "Now don't let no one tell you that you're no princess. You're most luverly, if you ask me," now looking at Hart, "I'm sure that your father would agree."

"Oh I agree, Sir," Hart replied.

The Capitalist remained silent returning his rather robust hat to his petite noggin.

"Follow me Mister Hart and bring with you your princess, and we shall go and see your Mister Morris," the captain said while disappearing back into the black hole.

# 10

The Capitalist and Hart followed Captain Johnson down a long narrow corridor. As they approached its end, Captain Johnson let out a yell. "Mister Morris!" He then made an unexpected hard right and entered the room. Hart and The Capitalist remained in the hall.

"'ello Mister Morris," Captain Johnson said.

"Yes," replied a soft but deep baritone voice from inside the cell.

"We have two visitors who say they are here to see you."

"Visitors?"

"A Mister Ephraim Hart and his luverly companion."

"I know of no Harts," said the voice.

"The visitors will please enter the cell," Captain Johnson ordered.

Hart and The Capitalist entered the cell. It looked to be about seven feet wide by ten feet long by ten feet high. Dust flowed forming ever-changing whirly patterns in the swath of light that entered by way of the highly positioned rectangular window hole. The place smelled of wet earth and sweet tobacco. Oddly comforting and manly. Standing next to the captain was a tall thick man with an enormous head. The captain dwarfed, his own head reaching only to the giant's belt buckle. He wore a beautifully tailored yellow suit with white stockings. But it was the head that was the thing of it. It was the largest on which Joel had ever laid eyes. The Capitalist was drawn to it like to chocolate cake or to the rounds of a man's buttocks—and immediately, he thought to himself, he was in the presence of a superior intellect. It was the first time that the prospect of a man's mind was the origin of a desire unspeakable. *Was this love?* The Capitalist asked himself as the warmth settled squarely into his tingly groins.

"I am surely grateful for this visit," the giant Morris said, "but I owe you both an apology, for I do not recall our ever having met. I do not owe you money, do I?"

"We've not ever met," replied The Capitalist, his eyes fixed on Morris's, his irises wobbled now darkened by desire and expanded pupils.

"I thought that you *knew* Mister Morris," said Captain Johnson.

"We do not know the man—but we know *of* him," Hart clarified.

"He does not owe us moneys, captain," said The Capitalist. "Rather, we seek Mister Morris's brains," adding, "We have come a long way."

"Brains?" asked Captain Johnson.

"Advice," said Hart. "I am Ephraim Hart," Hart continued, now extending his right hand to the giant Morris.

Morris took the hand, at which time Hart slid his thumb over the huge knuckle of Morris's equally huge index finger and applied pressure, Morris's face revealing that he had immediately recognized the grip.

"I hail," said Hart.

"I conceal?" whispered the giant in disbelief.

"Are you really going to do your knuckle shuffling here?" asked The Capitalist.

Hart again slid his thumb, this time to the knuckle of Morris's ridiculously huger middle finger and pressed.

"How do you like that?" Hart said.

"I'm confused," the giant murmured.

"I can do this all day," Hart said.

"Enough with the secret grips and tokens," said The Capitalist. "We're here for the man." The Capitalist's stare grew more intense.

Morris, confused though slightly aroused, returned the stare, though trying to get the upper hand of it.

The Capitalist eased up a bit on the staring, allowing the giant entry into his intentions. Sparkilating fireworks began to—

"Mister Morris?" interrupted the captain.

"Yes, captain, I agree to meet with these two... especially with this one," the giant said, staring at The Capitalist all the while.

"The knuckle molester too?" asked Captain Johnson.

"Yes, the knuckle molester too," answered Morris.

"You have thirty minutes," replied the captain, at which time he made an about face and exited the cell, making sure to perform the sharpest left turn that any princess had ever witnessed.

The giant sat down. Even so his torso towered over The Capitalist's tiny frame. Once convinced that no guards lurked outside the door, The Capitalist and Hart grew shoulder to shoulder, their bodies unintentionally bending toward the giant, as though drawn by the gravitational pull of the planetary mass of the giant's head.

"Tell me now of your magnificent canal venture," said The Capitalist while staring deeply into Morris's eyes. "I command it."

"I like where this is going," Mr. Morris replied.

# 11

"Where to begin," mused the giant. "There was the Panic of Seventeen Ninety-Six, of course, which is what ultimately brought me here. But, before that there was the Panic of Seventeen Ninety-Two, and the Crisis of Seventeen Ninety-One. There are several other such panics and crises—the Yazoo Land Fraud comes to mind. That was a whopper."

"Well," said Hart, "I should be interested in them all, but, alas, my tiny partner here is most interested in the orchestrated failure of your canal company."

"The Schuylkill and Susquehanna Navigation Company?" asked Morris.

"Is that the one?" Hart asked, looking to Joel.

"I ask only because there was also my Delaware and Schuylkill Canal Company."

"Which one failed by diabolic orchestration, the result of the Pennsylvania Act of Seventeen Ninety-One?," asked The Capitalist.

"Well, both companies fell in ruin due to that horrendous act," said Morris, "but it was the former company that failed due to the *diabolics* you so delicately mentioned."

"What act is this?" asked Hart, a bit confused.

"In Seventeen Ninety-One," answered The Capitalist softly, trance-like, monotone even, staring deeply into the giant's eyes, "an act was passed concerning the improvements of waterways, such as the Schuylkill and Susquehanna rivers here in Pennsylvania, which included legislation dealing with the building of canals that might also connect such rivers. You know...the whole lock-system thing? The aim of such improvements was to make the rivers passable upstream by installing a series of locks. Again, the lock-system thing. In many cases it was projected that improvements would require the assertion of *eminent domain* by the improving company. A great way to acquire capital at no cost to the improving company. Every capitalist's choice of acquisition if you ask me. But this act, this *horrendous* act, as my glorious giant just characterized it, made the easy acquisition of land difficult."

"*Gloriously* difficult, I'd say" Hart added.

"Impossible," corrected Morris. He continued as though taking the narrative baton from the dainty hands of The Capitalist, and in a trance-like, monotone manner began to run with it: "The act, this *horrendous* act as I am again characterizing it, since it pleases your partner in my characterizing it as such, required improvement companies to not only pay damages to owners of lands improved upon that were acquired through eminent domain, which would've been inconsequential since so few lands had been improved along those rivers, but it required companies to pay damages to owners of lands *not* improved upon!"

"That's a lot of land, I suspect," said Hart. "Rivers are quite long." He added, "It certainly is odd that companies that had seized land by eminent domain would have to pay owners for land that had *not* been developed. That doesn't give much incentive to the improvement companies to do any real work."

"And it gives none to capitalists," added The Capitalist.

"Aye, that was odd," replied the giant, his eyes still fixed on The Capitalist's. "I've been obsessively mulling this over since arriving here."

"About the length of rivers?" asked Hart.

"No, you idiot," the giant whispered, "My mullings have focused on the *identity* of the landowner." Then the giant broke briefly from his eyeing The Capitalist to glance at Hart, "Apologies for the *idiot*, but I've been under a lot of pressure lately."

"No apology necessary, my giant, for he *is* an idiot," whispered The Capitalist.

"Seriously, I am" added Hart, "my half-brother would tell you the same."

"You see," the giant continued, "originally the Schuylkill and Susquehanna Navigation Company was authorized to offer forty thousand shares in stock. No one investor was allowed to ever purchase or own more than ten. We even gifted George Washington a share just for good luck. Can you believe it? I took fifty-seven shares for myself as a way to secure that I would have more say in the future of the company. I don't believe that that was in violation of the mandate to limit ownership to ten. But I could be wrong. Who knows?"

"Well, everybody," said Hart. "I mean, fifty-seven is quite a bit larger than ten."

"Alright, you got me there. Maybe you're an idiot savant." Morris returned his eyes to The Capitalist's. "Trouble was, stock sales were slow going, where only a thousand had been sold." He sighed a healthy sigh. "Anyway, unbeknownst to me, my partner John Nicolson, stupid Johnny Nicolson, had been hard at work behind the scenes, even before the company was formed mind you, where he had been working to have that language about paying landowners for undeveloped lands put into the Seventeen Ninety-One Pennsylvania Act."

"Say more, my giant." pleaded The Capitalist.

"Stupid Johnny got around the mandate by not actually purchasing or owning the stock. You see, he had *borrowed* it. And so, technically speaking, he hadn't violated the limit of purchasing more than ten. Nonetheless he had in his possession two hundred and seventy shares. I discovered this and asked him about it, concerned that he would have more say than I with respect to the company's future. He replied that he valued the company so greatly that he just had to have more than ten stocks in his possession, but had no interest in the fact that he had more than I. He kept droning on about how he was really *into* the whole thing—and that I should concern myself about his zealous activities no longer. To show me that he was on the level he sold all his shares that day. And the douche really lucked out, for that day so happened to be the day our stocks would reach their greatest value."

"Sounds like he *was* into it." Hart said.

"He *was* into it alright, but not into it in the way one is into things normally," whispered the giant Morris, "But the thing on which to focus isn't that—on his being *into* it; the thing on which to focus is that he never *purchased* the stock, and so in a legal sense he had never purchased any stock. The money that he made when selling his shares was pure profit. He had *borrowed* the stock from the Treasurer of the company, stupid Tench Frances. Since he no longer possessed any stocks, he clearly was not in violation of the mandate. Brilliant, if you ask me. According to stupid Tench, stupid Johnny had promised to return the two hundred and seventy shares the following year. But that wasn't all. He had also promised to pay stupid Tench the price of the stock at the time he returned the stock. Stupid Tench, or *Stench* as I like to now call him, contracting 'stupid' and 'Tench,' clearly expected the stock price to *rise* over the year, and that once stupid Johnny had returned the stock, he'd simply sell it at its going price, while keeping stupid Johnny's payment for himself."

"*Stench*. That's a good one." said Hart.

"Seriously?" quipped The Capitalist, "that's the thing that arouses your interest?" He returned to the giant Morris: "So, stupid Johnny really didn't lose stock when the company went under?"

"No," replied the giant softly.

"How would stupid Johnny *know* that the company would fold before the deadline to repay the stock and extra payment arrived?"

"Oh, he knew," answered the giant.

"Was stupid Johnny psychical?" asked Hart with much dread. His jaw dropped a little.

"Before repaying Stench, after the stock had plummeted in value and he was able to purchase the stock at a really low price from another Broker—something like a penny a share, he gave the stock he had 'borrowed' back to Stench and paid him what they were now worth, which was pretty much nothing. Recall that he had sold the stock a year earlier, making much in the way of money. When he had returned those stocks to Stench, and paid him what they were then worth, which in all was only a bit over two dollars or so, he had made a great profit!"

"He got screwed." Hart said to The Capitalist.

"Aye," whispered The Capitalist.

"*Aye?* You never use the word *Aye*—" Hart chided.

"I do now," said The Capitalist staring intensely at the giant.

"Screwed?" asked the giant Morris.

"Yes," replied The Capitalist. "It expresses the notion that things have been made *much* worse by way of a turning of the screw."

"Harkens back to torture," Hart added with a smile, "you know, turning the screw?" As he said this he made a motion of holding a screwdriver and turning a screw.

"Good word," said the giant. "The notion seems fitting."

"I use only the best words and notions," whispered The Capitalist.

"*Your* word? You little baboon that's *my* word," said Hart.

"But this isn't the worst of it," sighed the giant Morris.

"I would think that that *was* the worst of it," said Hart, "I mean, it sounds as though you got screwed pretty good, to use *my* word that seems to please you both so much. But you've yet to reveal how stupid Johnny knew of the company's eventual fall. My vote is that he is psychical."

"I got screwed *plus some*," said the giant, ignoring Hart's request.

"Plus some? Tell me about this plus some," commanded The Capitalist.

"I shall. This *plus some*, as we're now calling it, is the answer to your query, Mister Hart," said the giant.

"Please relay it, then, this plus some." The Capitalist extended his tiny hand and cradled the giant's robust cheek. Some of the tension in the giant's face fell away.

"I feel like I'm in a dream," Hart said while taking in the show of affection.

"Please, Sir, tell us of the *plus some*. How could any man know such a thing as is being epistemically attributed to this stupid Johnny?" pleaded The Capitalist. "No man could know such things."

"Oh, he *knew* things, I will tell you that," replied the giant, "For, he had taken measures *himself* to assure that the stock's plummeting would manifest! It was no accident. And he is no prophet."

"The details!" commanded The Capitalist.

The giant's face responded, his eyes closing ever so gently, revealing an intense new pleasure, which surprisingly even to him arose from his being commanded in such ways. He replied: "Prior to engaging in his screwing, and before he had had that offensive language included in the Act, stupid Johnny had secretly acquired the land, or in other cases the rights to the land, that ran adjacent along both rivers, which was a simple matter, since most of the land was undeveloped and landowners had no qualms when it came to parting with it. They were also unaware of the soon to be legislated Act. As you'd expect, the owners would've believed that the land immediately along the rivers was useless, since it was, among other things, prone to seasonal flooding. They took it to be a godsend that anyone would offer them money for it or for the rights to it." said Morris.

"And what does this matter?" asked Hart with a tone.

"Don't you see," snapped The Capitalist, "it was also stupid Johnny who had secretly worked behind the scenes to have that language included in the Act, that anti-capitalist gibberish about compensating owners whose lands had been acquired through eminent domain, even those who had not developed their lands."

"Yes, and what—" Hart gasped, "—Oh, so the new Schuylkill and Susquehanna Navigation Company was unknowingly paying huge sums of company money to stupid Johnny?"

The giant nodded in affirmation. "The company could not recover from that expenditure. The hope of any future profit fell, and the stock value sunk to new lows each day. Despite appearing to be an investor,

Stupid Johnny had secured a means to decreasing the stock value and yet had profited from it."

"*Plus some*, indeed" said The Capitalist.

"I'm now more convinced than ever," said the giant, "that more people were in on it than just stupid Johnny. Probably that jackass Gouverneur Morris was one."

"Governor...I don't know of a Governor Morris." said Hart.

"No, it's pronounced *Gooveneer*. Can you believe it? He is such a pretentious ass," said Morris. "Lost his leg in a carriage accident."

"Morris? Your relation?" asked Hart.

"Heavens no, thank the gods! He's a real slimy one-legged bastard that one. You could make a visit to him if you're looking to learn how to *really* screw people, but I think that he is currently serving as a minister to France. Though I did hear rumor that the French really don't like him and that he was being shipped back to the United States."

The Capitalist made a mental note of it.

# 12

Hart and Joel met Uncle Yusuf just outside the Tontine Coffee House. It was abuzz. The Capitalist had never been to the place, having only heard about it from Hart. The boy found the naked orgy of trading and exchanging of money intoxicating.

"Nephew," shouted Yusuf while extending his tree-trunk-like arms out preparing for an embrace. He took hold of Joel and rocked him back and forth in a bear hug.

"He goes by *The Capitalist* these days," Hart said.

"Capitalist?" Yusuf replied, looking down into Joel's eyes.

"*The* Capitalist," corrected Hart.

"*The Capitalist*? What is this about?" asked Yusuf.

"Amassing capital," The Capitalist confidently asserted, looking up at his uncle.

"Amassing capital..." Yusuf repeated as his eyes shifted to Hart.

"Let's grab a table," said Hart.

"Looks busy," Yusuf assessed.

"Looks like Heaven," The Capitalist said.

"Okay, let's grab a table," Yusuf sang, his massive brown paws releasing The Capitalist, though only to take him by the shoulder as they entered the building.

Hart spied a table in the corner. Joel's eyes widened. The noise reminded him of what he imagined it would be like to be inside a great machine as its heavy pistons pounded away. The energy of the room overwhelmed him. His face grew pleasantly warm as his eyes teared up. The largest smile he ever smiled tightened his already reddened cheeks. He knew that not even the holiest of ancient temples had ever matched the spectacle of the Tontine Coffee House.

They sat.

"Coffee?" Yusuf asked.

"Yes," Hart replied.

"Coffee?" Yusuf asked Joel.

"Do I like coffee?" The Capitalist asked Hart.

"How should I know?" Hart replied.

"No way to know until you try it," said Uncle Yusuf.

"Okay,...Coffee," The Capitalist said.

"With sugar and hot cream; you'll like that," Yusuf added.

Through a noisy sea of well-dressed seated men Uncle Yusuf slowly navigated his wide frame toward the busy counter on the other side of the large space.

"So this is the Tontine Coffee House," said Joel.

"It is," Hart said, his eyes surveying the room.

Joel noticed how different his stepfather appeared when sitting among the men that populated his everyday work life. This had not revealed itself at home or during their travels. He had somehow managed to hide this aspect of himself. Something about this place he thought brought out something quite manly in both Hart and Yusuf. They were clearly respected and even appeared wise. He felt safe with Hart and his Uncle Yusuf. No harm could come to him in their presence he thought. Strange that he had not noticed this before.

# 13

So, you say we have two thousand shares to sell?" Uncle Yusuf asked. He carefully lowered to the table what appeared to be three large white bowls of hot caramel cream. The aroma was deep and thrilling. The bowls had handles; no doubt to be used as large cups.

"Two thousand," Hart confirmed.

"It may be a challenge to move that many this morning," Yusuf said.

"So we're doing this here?" asked The Capitalist.

"Yes, such doings happen here," said Hart.

"I queried Harold Simmons and he says that as of this morning the stock is selling for three dollars and forty-six cents per script," Yusuf reported.

"That's nineteen cents more than when we acquired the stock from Mister Carmichael," The Capitalist said. His huge smile grew huger.

"I know, right?" Hart said with glee. "You sure we want to do this? I mean, maybe we just keep the stock and see how high it goes. Sell it in a few weeks from now."

"No, we need to sell them as soon as possible," replied The Capitalist. "We only got six months to bring ruin to the Western Inland Lock Navigation Company. The sooner we sell the stock, the sooner we can get to the ruin thing. My worry is that the longer we hold on to the stock the more risk we run."

"Ruin?" asked Yusuf.

"Yes, our little genius has a plan. I told you about it all last night," Hart reminded.

"This is that?" Yusuf said.

"This is that," Hart confirmed.

Hart renewed his efforts at surveying the room. He held Joel's forearm and gave it a comforting squeeze. "I think that we can move the stock today if we sell it for less than what it's going for, which your uncle says is three-forty-six. Let's price it at what it was going for when we acquired it—three-twenty-seven. What do you think?"

"That's a loss of nineteen cents per share. Multiply that by two thousand and we're talking a loss of three hundred and eighty dollars," said The Capitalist.

"Okay, so we'll open with today's price, but I'm betting that no one will bite until we make it worth their while. It's a lock company for Petessakes."

"Yes, this is not a well-known company let alone a well-known script, my nephew," Yusuf added.

"Fine. Let's start at today's price and if no one is buying we can drop it. But no lower than three-twenty-seven, got it?" The Capitalist demanded.

"Got it O Sahib," confirmed Hart.

"*Sahib*...nice!" added Uncle Yusuf. He sipped his coffee. It was exceptionally robust this morning. "I am concerned, I must admit," he continued, "about your plans to ruin the company. Why must you do that? Did this company do anything to offend you?"

"No, of course not. I don't even know what a lock company does really," said Hart. "Well, that's not true. I know that they construct structures that can temporarily block the seaward flow of a river so that a ship can move *up*river. But neither the kid nor I have been harmed by this company."

"My faith will not allow me to participate in any of the harm you may be planning," said Yusuf more seriously than usual.

"Rest assured, Uncle," said The Capitalist, "the stocks you are selling represent a healthy company—well, as far as you know. I mean, look at the rise in their value. We had nothing to do with that. So, today you are selling stock on the up and up. *You* are not participating in producing any harm."

"Clearly the boy has been hanging out with you far too much. When does his mother return?" Yusuf asked.

"Her most recent letter says February," Hart said.

"So five months?"

"Five long months," Hart confirmed. He missed Frances very much.

Yusuf put his hand on Joel's. "But, my bright nephew, I *am* aware of your intentions to do harm, where part of your plan is the selling of these stocks. So, I feel that I am a conspirator of sorts even if I do not participate in the harm you plan to do later."

"Understood," The Capitalist said, "but perhaps your feelings of future guilt will be diminished in knowing that the odds of your brother and I having the competence to do said harm are pretty low." Joel did not believe this himself but thought that it would comfort his uncle.

"He's got a point," added Hart.

"True," Yusuf said, "I love the both of you, but I would not wager a penny on the proposition that you will succeed."

Uncle Yusuf's well-stated concern was even beginning to shake The Capitalist's confidence in the plan a little.

Yusuf continued, "Why did you choose this company for your plan anyway? It would seem to me that there are other companies that might better fit your plans."

"Your brother and I had learned from a disgruntled employee that although it was putting its best face forward the company was unraveling and was bordering on failure in its current project," said The Capitalist.

"Current project?" Yusuf asked.

"The company has been contracted by the state of New York to build a lock system along the Mohawk River," replied The Capitalist.

"And that's not going well?" asked Yusuf.

"Correct," The Capitalist said. "We learned from this former employee that they were retooling the company's image which included their engineering a lot of 'good' press. But it's all propaganda.

They are using the ruse in the newspapers to raise capital. This probably accounts for the current rise in stock value."

"Maybe you can feel better about all this," Hart added, "knowing that the company is evil and our bringing it down is really a good."

"Maybe," entertained Yusuf. "But now I feel even worse knowing that the current value of the stock is built on lies."

"Don't be so naïve my good uncle, all market value is built on lies" said The Capitalist in his monotone voice.

"We have to find you a girl," said Uncle Yusuf.

"Not necessary," Hart said, "he's already got himself a boyfriend. His glorious giant. Tell your good uncle about your giant."

Yusuf looked puzzled.

Hart reminded The Capitalist, "Remember that the three of us are partners in this. We split the profits equally, even if your uncle's work ends with selling these stocks. We must honor his faith."

"Agreed," said The Capitalist.

"Seriously," said Yusuf, "tell me of this giant."

# 14

The face of the magnificent giant stared deeply into Joel's eyes. The young man's body vibrated. His tiny heart pounded...Bang! Bang! Bang!

"Who on earth could that be?" Joel heard Hart say. "It's still dark."

The pounding sounded again. It was coming from the front door downstairs.

Hart and Joel had been sound asleep. Their efforts to sell the two thousand stocks had been a success. However, the effort had cost them three long days. Hart put on his robe and scurried out of the room down the stairs.

The door pounded again.

"Hold your horses, I'm on my way," shouted Hart from the foyer.

"Brother?" someone whispered from behind the door. It sounded like Yusuf.

Hart opened the door. It *was* Yusuf! He stood there in a woman's robe, though he had gone to the trouble of donning his leather man-boots. He carried a flickering lantern, which looked like a child's, the thing dwarfed by his massive hand. He could see Yusuf's carriage outside.

"Brother," repeated Yusuf out of breath, "I have good news for you...well, perhaps bad...I am not sure. But I think it's good."

"Come in come in," Hart insisted. Yusuf quickly entered.

Hart shut the door and the two stood facing one another in their robes. Joel stood about halfway up the staircase, looking down on his father and uncle standing in the foyer. He had on Frances' robe that Hart had given her as a birthday gift—it was mesmerizingly ornate, made in France of course. They each stared heavily at one another's attire.

"Let me put on some water. Tea?" Hart said.

"Coffee if you have it," Yusuf replied.

"Coffee," Hart acknowledged.

"The grinder is on top of the cabinet," Joel yawned while rubbing his eyes.

"What news brings you here so early?" Hart asked as he disappeared into the kitchen. He reached for the grinder and put it on the table. "Joel, can you hang the kettle and get the hot water going?" He glanced at the fire in the great room. "The fire's looking a bit scant. Take care of that. Make sure to stoke it. Open the flew a bit more so you don't smoke us out."

"I know how to do it," Joel said.

"Where's that linen bag your mother uses to steep the coffee grounds?" Hart called from the kitchen.

"It should be next to the grinder," Joel called back.

"I take it that you two don't use the kitchen much with your mother gone," Yusuf queried.

"We like the chicken pie at Fighting Cocks," Joel answered.

"Yes, good chicken pie, I agree," said Yusuf.

Hart reappeared from the kitchen. "What's the news?"

"I was at the Tontine Coffee House and..."

"I thought that you went home last night when we did," Hart interrupted.

"No," said Yusuf. He paused, then continued, "I sometimes stay there all night."

"The Tontine Coffee House is open *all night*?" Joel asked.

"It is," answered Uncle Yusuf, "business never sleeps."

"Were you wearing just your robe?" asked Hart confused.

"This isn't mine. It's Misses Tontine's. She was doing my laundry," Yusuf replied matter-of-factly.

"Your laundry," Hart said in disbelief.

Yusuf shrugged his shoulders. "What?"

"Go on, go on," Hart insisted, "the news..."

"I was at the Tontine Coffee House, and a post arrived for Simmons updating him on stock prices and whatnot, which he receives daily, and I believe it includes information that the Western Inland Lock Navigation Company has filed papers and looks to be going under. Well, I *know* that the post includes this. I got a peek at it..."

"While Misses Tontine was doing your laundry," Hart paused, then asked, "What do you mean *going under*?"

"Kaput" said Yusuf, his hands making the gesture of a great explosion.

"My goodness," said Hart, "to think that we held two thousand units not three days ago."

"I suspect some will be a bit angry at you after having purchased the stock," said Yusuf.

"Me?" Hart said, "you mean *us*?"

"Well, buyers know that I was working *for you*. I'm not a stockjobber, like you who is one," Yusuf said.

"What *do* you do, uncle? Workwise, I mean," asked Joel.

"I'm a businessman," Yusuf said.

"That's pretty general," Joel replied. He immediately looked at Hart. "Don't!" he said sternly.

"I didn't say anything," Hart said. He looked at Yusuf. "They'll know that there's no way that anyone could have known that this was going to happen."

"Can you get into trouble?" Joel asked. "I thought that if a company goes under that you don't suffer any consequences."

"I don't," Hart said.

"So what are you saying, uncle?" Joel asked.

"Your uncle is saying that we don't have to head north today," Hart answered.

"What about the money?" Joel The Capitalist asked.

"What about it? We keep it," Hart confirmed. "We didn't do anything illegal."

"And luckily you probably didn't do anything immoral either. At least the fall of the company did not come at *your* hands," Yusuf said, "even though secretly you were hoping for its fall."

"Wanting something isn't illegal," Hart asserted.

"That's good to hear. I want bad things to happen to others all the time," said The Capitalist.

Hart began cranking the grinder's handle. The room filled with a pungently sweet aroma as the roasted beans were ground to dust. "Even if the company completely goes under, we'll still have to visit Mister Carmichael," he said.

"Why?" The Capitalist asked, "The company is kaput. You heard Uncle Yusuf. The stock is worth nothing!"

"Technically, not *nothing*. So long as the company legally exists and is registered with the market the stock price can get low, as low as a fraction of a penny, but a share will not be worth *nothing*," said Hart. "Besides, we still have six months to go. Things could turn around for our Western Inland Lock Navigation Company."

"The company can recover?" asked The Capitalist.

"If they secured financing," answered Uncle Yusuf. "And given the money they must have made from recent stock sales; they might have recovered already. News may not travel so fast to Simmons. For all we know, tomorrow's post will say that the company has recovered and is back on its feet."

"Yes," Hart paused, playing the thing out in his head. "This morning's update could be at least two days off." He thought some more. "I'm afraid that we'll just have to head north after all...We'll need to make sure that the knocked-down company stays down for the count."

"Let it lie," Yusuf pleaded.

"Look...we don't have to *harm* the company directly," Hart said. "We just need to make sure that their situation doesn't improve. We just need to politely ask them to stay down. You know, for their own sake?"

"So we're still going?" The Capitalist said, the corners of his mouth moving slightly upward.

"Yes, we're still going," Hart answered. "We'll leave this morning. We can be there in two days."

"Take my carriage," Yusuf said.

"Well, that would take more than two days. But I'll take you up on the carriage, for it needn't take us very far. I've already booked passage for me, you, and the monkey there to *sail* upriver. Quicker. It'll take only two days." Hart paused and then asked, "What, you're not coming?"

"Heavens no, brother," Yusuf said.

"Maybe that's for the best," Hart added, "you can stay here and smooth over any concerns that may arise after Simmons sees the post. You can put it around to interested parties that I have personally headed north to see about the company. Technically, that's not a lie."

"I can do that," agreed Yusuf. "But you have to promise me that you will not commit any sins in which I would be implicated through association."

"Fine. Though I suspect that if we *have* to do any sinning, we can make sure to do the lesser ones," Hart assured.

"Are there lesser ones?" Yusuf asked.

"Which sin is lesser, my Muslim brother, greed or fraud?" Hart answered with a question.

"Well, if we accept Dante's ranking, I would say that greed is the lesser," answered Yusuf.

"Who's Dante?" The Capitalist asked.

"See? *Lesser*," Hart said. He paused and then turned to Joel, "Committing the sin of greed puts one in the fourth circle of Hell, whereas the sin of fraud puts one in the eighth," Hart filled the linen bag with the fragrant grounds.

"The eighth is the worst," Yusuf assured Joel.

"Who's Dante?" The Capitalist repeated. "Have I met him?"

"So, perhaps we can direct our wills motivated by greed instead of fraud," Hart concluded.

"Neither can be *my* motivation, brother," assured Yusuf, "My motivation can only remain my loyalty I have to you. We are partners in this. If greed is *your* motive, that is none of my business, though I counsel against it." He paused and then said, "Weigh your actions carefully. I do not wish to have to visit you two in Hell."

"Hell?" The Capitalist asked. "I thought that greed was *the* motivator of a capitalist. If it's founded on something *evil*, I am surprised that it has been so widely adopted by our fellow Christian citizens, who so pompously profess to be among the elected."

"This is a mystery, I admit," said Yusuf.

"I prefer to think that the motivation of a capitalist is *success*," Hart interjected. "I can hear the water boiling," he said to Joel.

"Boiling?" asked Joel.

"The kettle..." Hart replied, motioning to the fireplace.

"But greed can mask for the pursuit of success, no?" Yusuf proffered.

"I propose that we table the discussion of sins, drink some coffee, and figure out what we might do up north that will not send my son and me to Hell," Hart said.

This was the first time that Joel could recall hearing Hart's referring to him as his son.

# 15

The sloop arrived at the port of Albany about six in the evening. It was late summer and there was plenty of sunlight left. It was warm and wet and the tall trees along the river formed a vibrant deep green curtain. The rhythm of the cicadas rose and fell, providing a kind of calm to this otherwise lively stage. Stoves being readied for dinner filled the air with the sweet smell of hickory.

Hart had been instructed by his friend Leonard Bleeker, a cosigner of the Buttonwood Agreement, that once in Albany to go to Lion Street, just off the Public Square, where a few blocks up he should find lodging at the Iron Horse Tavern.

Hart and The Capitalist disembarked from the sloop and ventured over to the freight building, where they could retrieve their trunk that had been put in the ship's cargo hold. Joel had tucked under his arm his uncle's copy of the first book of Dante's *Divine Comedy*, *The Inferno*. An impressive schooner sat in the harbor. It must have ported long before their small ship had arrived, and it now looked to be uploading cargo. Hart had noted that usually ships of that size would not venture this far upriver. Joel overheard men talking about the ship's being prepared for its return to the Netherlands, the large wooden crates filled with pelts, a product of the region's fur trade.

To bide the time, Joel perused what seemed like a thousand papers posted on an exterior wall of the warehouse that apparently served as a local kiosk. One post immediately caught his attention, though the bulk of it lay hidden under several layers of partially overlapping papers. The exposed part read:

TEN DOLLARS Reward. RUN AWAY on Friday the 26th of August 1774, from the subscriber, living in Middle-patent, North-Castle, Westchester county, and province of New York. A NEGRO MAN, Named WILL, about 27 years of age, about five feet six inches high, somewhat of a yellow complexion, a spry lively fellow, very talkative; had on when he went away, a butter-nut coloured coat, felt hat, tow cloth trowsers; he has part of his right ear cut off, and a mark on the backside of his right hand. Whoever takes up said Negro and brings him to his master, or secures him in gaol, so that his master may have him again, shall have the above reward and all reasonable charges, paid by JAMES BANKS. N.B. Masters of vessels are hereby warned not to carry off the above Negro.

The date of the post and its buried location showed that it had to be over twenty years old. It didn't look like anyone ever took these things down. He wondered whether the man who was missing a hunk of his ear had ever been found and returned to James Banks.

There were more enslaved people in Albany County than in any other in New York—though this was rivaled by Brooklyn, where one-third of its population was enslaved. In the city of Albany, there were about 600 slaves. Only 26 or so people of African descent living in the city were free. Hart had mentioned all of this to Joel as a way of preparing him for the likely prospect of their encountering a much larger number of slaves than he was used to seeing in their isolated neighborhood in New York City.

Hart had once told Joel of a rather significant slave market that had operated at the end of Wall Street near the East River. It had vanished mysteriously about fifteen years before Joel was born. One in three blacks in New York City were free men. He had actually never met any former slaves. Hart and Frances did not like the reality of slavery, but the only remedy they could muster in response to it was to ignore it. This strategy had worn off on Joel. Blacks and whites kept to themselves and did not often engage one another on the streets.

So, there were few opportunities for white and black boys to become friends.

Joel had overheard Hart and Yusuf once discussing a new law passed by the New York state legislature that said that slaves born after that July would be considered *legally* free, though they would have to serve as indentured servants until they were in their twenties. Once they had reached the designated age, they were free. Hart and Yusuf agreed that this was a step in the right direction.

Another post caught Joel's attention:

> TO BE SOLD, A servant woman acquainted with both city and country business, about 30 years of age, and sold because she wishes to change her place. Enquire at 91 Cherry-Street.

This seemed just ridiculous, Joel thought—was this servant woman really up for sale because *she* wanted a change of place? He didn't for a second believe that any slave would have that sort of say as to where they lived and worked. A host of other such politely written posts that cast slaves as disgruntled employees littered the kiosk. If this were evidence of anything, it was that slavery was still a significant source of labor in the new nation, and that many New Yorkers were pretending otherwise.

Joel had understood his new religion of capitalism to require several things, probably the most important being a free market. The second most important thing was that a capitalist owns the means of production. This included ownership and control over materials and labor. Slavery, it had seemed to Joel at the time, was *the* archetype of owning and controlling labor. It made the ownership of labor the same as the ownership of materials. Joel had reasoned to himself that a *free* market was a market that would allow the selling and buying of *anything*—*no* regulations—where, conceptually speaking anyway, the selling and buying of human beings would be just a part of the selling and buying of anything.

He saw what appeared to be a more recent post. It advertised a need for laborers, for the Western Inland Navigation Lock Company's project to construct a canal and lock system up the Mohawk River. Although a corner of the post had been torn away, from what remained of the date it appeared that the advertisement was posted sometime this year. Interested parties could inquire at a table located in the Public Square market.

# 16

"There's our trunk," Joel said. He heard laughter come from the direction of the large schooner. It sounded like it included the voice of a young man. He looked but saw no one.

Hart looked around the busy warehouse, his palms placed against his lower back that worked to push his hips forward. The stretch felt good. "Let's see if we can find someone to deliver it to the tavern," he said. He asked a man who looked like he knew his way around. "Sir, is there someone with whom I can speak to arrange delivering this trunk to the Trojan Horse Tavern?"

"Tom's yur man," said the man. "Tom!" he yelled as though looking through Hart.

"Here!" called a young man's voice from somewhere behind Hart.

"This gent requires yer services," the man shouted.

"Be right there," Tom said.

The laughter came again. This time Joel spied several men on the deck of the schooner. There was in fact a boy among them. The boy scouted Joel and waved. Joel didn't know what to do but before he could consider the matter any further, he found himself smiling and waving back out of habit.

"Sir," said Tom to Hart, "How may I be of service?" Tom was at least a foot taller than Joel. He looked to be about sixteen or seventeen years old. He was lean and muscular. His smile revealed a healthy set of white teeth, accentuated by his dark skin. He wiped off his hand with a rag and extended it to Hart.

Hart took his hand. Strong grip. "What would it cost to have you deliver this trunk to the Trojan Horse Tavern?" he asked.

"Twenty-five cents," Tom replied. "We have an Iron Horse Tavern. There is no Trojan Horse Tavern."

"Oh, the *Iron* Horse. Very good, the Iron Horse Tavern," Hart said. "Why would I say *Trojan Horse*? We will go ahead then and expect the trunk's delivery by nightfall. The *Iron* Horse Tavern!"

"I can have it there within the hour," Tom said, looking at Joel.

"Should I pay now?" Hart asked while looking for his purse.

"No, Sir," Tom said, "After the trunk is delivered.

"Very good then" Hart said.

Tom extended his hand to Joel, "Tom."

"Yes, how rude of me," Hart said to Tom, "this is my son, Joel."

Joel took Tom's hand and shook it. The image of his father's attempts at knuckle-shuffling with the giant came to mind. Tom was much younger than his giant and, if it were even possible, more handsome.

"Very good," Hart said. "Off to the Iron Horse Tavern."

# 17

The Public Square was busier than Joel had expected. Several merchants continued to do business under a large, tented area. Even so, most of the tables stood empty. No doubt tomorrow the place would be bustling with the merchants of Albany. Children chased one another, weaving in and out of the maze of abandoned tables. Joel looked for the Western Inland Navigation Lock Company. But the only merchants that remained appeared to be several farmers selling corn.

"Lion Street!" shouted Joel to Hart. "Do you see the sign?"

"I see *a* sign," Hart admitted. "Can you actually read it from here?"

"Yes, old man," Joel replied.

⋇⋇⋇

The Iron Horse Tavern smelled surprisingly clean. The large windows were open, and a fragrant breeze moved through the building. The planked wooden floor and simple furniture were immaculately oiled. The curtains and various throw rugs smelled like freshly starched cotton.

Once in the large foyer, Hart and The Capitalist had a bead on every adjacent downstairs room. The dining room was to the left, a sitting room to the right. Straight ahead was a large staircase that went up at a rather steep pitch. It was wide enough to accommodate four adults and a horse. Hallways framed each side of the staircase, through which staff hurriedly moved. A clatter of kitchen staff could be heard coming from behind the massive staircase.

A wildly overdressed man emerged from the dining room.

"Welcome to the Iron Horse," he said. "May I assist you?"

"Why, yes," Hart said with a wide smile, "I am Ephraim Hart and this is my son Joel Hart, and we have it on the highest recommendation to seek lodging at your establishment. I sent word by letter two days ago to alert you of our arrival. I do hope that you received it."

"I do not recall having received such a post, Mister Hart, but the day's mail will arrive within the hour. Perhaps it shall arrive then."

The three stared at one another for a moment as if waiting for the other shoe to drop.

"Well," Hart said, breaking the entranced moment, "I hope that you can accommodate us even though my advanced request for a room has yet to arrive."

"Yes, Mister Hart," the man said, "We can register you and your son and place you in a room."

They again fell into an episode of staring at one another.

"Very good?" Hart said, hoping that this would serve as the other shoe.

"Very good," replied the man. He gave a slight bow and then disappeared through one of the narrow hallways.

"Should we follow him?" Joel asked.

"I am not sure," Hart replied. "I am a bit confused."

"Good. For a moment I thought it was just me," said Joel.

The man returned with a large ledger and invited them to sit at the dining table in the other room while he filled out the necessary registry entries.

"Tea?" the man asked.

"No, thank you," Hart answered.

As the man gathered the necessary information from Hart, Joel felt a change of air pressure in the room and saw a rectangle of light grow across the floor of the foyer. A shadow of a man occupied its center. It was Tom. He was carrying a canvas bag over his shoulder and wheeled in their trunk, which he had secured atop a flat dolly.

"That was fast," said Joel.

Tom saw Hart and Joel sitting at the dining table with Mr. Wrench. He smiled at Joel when their eyes met.

Mr. Wrench looked up from his ledger and stood to address Tom. "Good, I see that the mail has arrived."

"Yes, Sir," Tom confirmed as he handed the canvas bag to Mr. Wrench. "It came on the very ship that brought these two gentlemen."

"Seriously?" said Hart with some embarrassment.

Mr. Wrench put the bag on the table, opened it, and produced a letter. "Is this your letter, Mister Hart?"

"Yup," Hart said.

Mr. Wrench opened it and silently read the entire thing.

"You see, I was telling the truth..." Hart said with a fake laugh.

Mr. Wrench put the letter back into its envelope. He produced from his pocket a coin and gave it to Tom.

"That reminds me," Hart said as he stood, "I should settle up with you, Tom." He found his purse in his coat, shook it so as to produce the sound of clinking coins, opened it and gave Tom a quarter dollar. "I believe that is what we agree to?"

"Yes, Sir," said Tom. "Thank you very much."

"No, no, thank *you*," Hart said.

"I can take the trunk to your rooms if you like," Tom offered.

"No need," said Mr. Wrench, "our staff can handle it from here."

Joel detected some tension between the two men. But it was short-lived, as Hart and Mr. Wrench sat and returned to the ledger.

"So," Joel said to Tom, "you work at the freight warehouse."

"Yes," Tom said.

An awkward pause.

"Looks like a lot of work," Joel said.

"It is," Tom said, "but it can be fun too."

"Fun?"

"Well, not *fun* really," Tom admitted. He composed a new thought. "I will be starting a new job, it won't be my *main* job, but a second or third job, but I'll be keeping this one, at least a while longer, and that third job looks like it may actually be fun."

"Oh yeah?" Joel said with interest. "You got a lot of jobs."

"Yeah. I'll be working weekends for a fancy engineering company that has taken to building a canal and lock system up the Mohawk."

"Really?!?" Joel lit up. His heart raced.

"If you'll be in town for a bit, maybe I could show you around the warehouse and take you to the canal site? The trench they've already dug is ridiculously impressive. You could fit all of Lion Street into it, buildings and all. I am not kidding."

"I would like it very much to go to those places with you," said Joel in the most serious adult voice he could muster.

# 18

Joel awoke to a subtle but growing aroma of frying bacon. Lightly pounding footsteps could be heard working their way passed their room's door toward the grand staircase. Murmuring voices and tinkling glasses and a cacophony of metal forks and knives dropping onto ceramic plates grew more pronounced.

The door to their room opened. It was Hart. The Capitalist had not noticed that his father had gotten out of bed and that he lay there alone. Hart had a white towel wrapped around his neck and smelled of witch-hazel.

"Why don't you get cleaned up," Hart said. "We will get breakfast downstairs. Smells good."

"Okay," Joel said. "I don't know if you overheard my conversation with Tom last night, but he says that he'll be working on Saturday for our lock company."

"Is that so?" Hart replied with widened eyes.

"He said he would take me where they've begun digging the canal."

"That's serendipitous," Hart noted, "It's Thursday, so we'll have two days to scout things out before you go."

"It's Friday," Joel corrected.

"Friday? It is? How'd that happen?" Hart asked.

"You know, usually follows Thursday," Joel said. "What's *serendipitous* mean?"

"It means that seemingly random events have aligned to our advantage," Hart answered. "So we have *one* day to scout things out. Still serendipitous if you ask me."

"Tom said I can meet him around ten this morning at the warehouse," Joel added. "What time is it now?"

"Perhaps you can get some information on whether our lock company's supply line runs through the warehouse. You know, like I said, scout things out?" He opened the door and leaned some ways out into the hallway. Joel heard him politely greet a passerby. He leaned back into the room and closed the door. "Clock says it's six twenty-eight."

"Plenty of time," Joel said. "Good idea about the scouting thing." It was tautological that any plan that included another encounter with the beautiful Tom was a good idea, serendipitous or not.

"You must admit that I get a good one every now and again," Hart replied.

"You might even say that getting them was serendipitous," Joel said.

# 19

"Excuse me, Sir," Joel said to a sweaty man sweeping the floor. "Do you know where I might find Tom?"

"I'm over here," yelled a voice from behind a massive stack of crates. Tom appeared from around the mammoth structure. He carried a thick rope.

He was more beautiful than Joel had earlier recalled.

"Thank you for letting me do this," Joel said. "It is very considerate of you."

"My pleasure," Tom said with a tone that assured Joel that he had meant it.

"So, you're a stevedore, right?" Joel asked.

"Yes," Tom said a bit surprised.

"The name is about all I know really," Joel admitted. "I asked Mister Wrench about you."

Tom rolled his eyes. "I wouldn't put too much stock in what he says about me. But he's right about the job title."

"So, what's a stevedore?" Joel queried.

"A stevedore downloads and uploads cargo. Cargo is stored in a warehouse like this or in a stockyard. I'm still an apprentice, so I only work in the warehouse and stockyard for now. Eventually I'll join the downloaders and uploaders out on the dock."

"I was watching those men. Looks dangerous," Joel said as he peered out at the men holding ropes that traveled through large pulleys, several men barking orders at the others.

"Dangerous for sure," Tom said in a serious tone. "Easy for a man to get killed. Crushed to death mostly."

"Crushed. Yes, I can see how that could happen."

"Like a pancake."

"Have you ever witnessed such a pancaking?" Joel asked.

"No. Thank goodness. But it has happened," Tom confirmed. "The most recent was a few years before I got here. Mostly I've seen only crushed fingers." He could see how the report of all the crushing was affecting Joel. Tom smiled and changed the subject. "When ships port here, their cargo is either set in this building or out in the stockyard to be distributed to the surrounding area, and then from there to who knows where. Or it is set to be loaded aboard another ship to be carried south, almost always all the way south to the New York City ports, and then out across the Atlantic on really large ships." He put the heavy rope down. "We sort cargo out according to type. Most of what you see here in crates is what we call *break bulk*. Over on that side of the warehouse you'll find bundles of lumber, steel rods, and the like. They are what we call *neo bulk*. Over there in those barrels are all sorts of liquids—mostly oil for lanterns and such. That's called *liquid bulk*. Dry bulk is over there in that corner. You'll find coal, iron ore, sand, and what not there."

"So, a system of *bulks*," Joel said. "Interesting."

"Bulks," Tom laughed.

"Are you done loading the big schooner?" Joel asked.

"Almost. Takes about a week to load something that big."

"I heard that its cargo is precious furs," Joel said.

"Yes," Tom said, "I heard that too."

"What's that building?" Joel asked, pointing to a blue-washed building nearer the dock.

"That's the counting house," Tom replied, "All of the inventory and financials are recorded there."

"And that building?" Joel continued, pointing to the building next to the counting house.

"That's..."

A short, aggressive man fell upon the two boys.

"We're ready for the galley stock." he barked.

"There," Tom said, pointing to a mass of stacked jute bags. The man turned and marched to the monstrous mass. Tom looked at Joel. "I must go. Why don't you take a look around. Stay clear of the dock and definitely stay clear of any working ropes. If they snap, you could be cut in half."

"Half!" Joel said a bit louder than he intended and then gulped.

"Like Solomon's baby," Tom said. "Find me at lunch time."

"That's one pushy man," He looked at the barking douche who had interrupted his time with Tom. The image of the sergeant at Prune Street Prison flashed before his mind's eye, the tiny sergeant cut in half by a snapped rope.

"Speaking of that schooner, that's its chandler," Tom said. "He *is* pushy. Must go. Don't want him getting any pushier."

"I'll find you for lunch," Joel confirmed. "I'll try not to get crushed."

"Don't forget cut in half!" Tom yelled as he disappeared between stacks of crates.

# 20

Joel had some time to kill before meeting back up with Tom. He took a stroll through the marketplace. It was noticeably hotter than earlier that morning when he had set out for the warehouse. As he had thought, the market was a bustling center of Albany. The throng of marketgoers sounded like a cacophony of scavenging gulls. The summer air was sweet, infused with the aroma of hickory smoke from a pit set up behind a butcher's table.

Near the market's center was in fact a table at which the Western Inland Lock Navigation Company had set up a recruiting station. Joel felt victorious, his faculty of forming expectations had again prevailed! Several young men stood around the table taking in the fevered sermon given by a rotund, pink-faced man with large grey muttonchops. He was dressed in black, wearing a large black hat. On the table sat what Joel surmised was a wooden model of one of the company's locks. Joel thought it a good idea to mosey over to the theatrical performance and spy said model.

He felt a curious tug from the back of his shirt.

"Hallo," said the tugger to Joel. It was the boy from the ship, the one who had waved to him! He looked much taller up close, older too, and his skin was even warmer and browner than he had remembered it. The bold young man sported a wildly curly hairdo. He held a skewer-stick that supported the weight of a magnificently plump still-sizzling sausage.

"It's you!" Joel said. "Do you member me?"

"O corse I do," he said right in the middle of taking a big bite of the sausage. "Why else will a mon be tugging you on you blouse."

"You talk...," Joel stopped mid-sentence correcting course, "I like your accent."

"I ama from Espania. My Englich is no so good."

"Well, it's better than my Spanish," Joel replied.

"¿Tú hablas español?" he asked with eyes widened.

"I'm sorry,...what's that?" Joel asked.

"Supongo que eso seria no," he said to himself while taking the sticked sausage in one hand and wiping the palm of the other on his pantaloons.

"So, that's Spanish I take it?"

"Sí. I mean, *jes*. Thot es espanich," he said. "You leeb here?"

"No, just visiting. You?"

"Bisiteen *mi*? How ju bisiteen mi? I leeb on dee sheep. I no leeb here. Ju make joke, no?"

"Sorry. I meant to ask whether you were visiting too? I was being polite. I figured that you were not from around here."

"I from Espania. I already tolded ju. Dees es no Espania. O corse I bisiteen," the boy said.

"Yes, that makes sense."

"My name es Ignacio López de Ayala. I am nameed ofter...how ju say...*mi abuelo*?" he extended his free hand, "Barry nice to met ju."

Joel took his hand. "Very nice to meet you, Ignacio. My name is Joel Hart. I don't think I was named after anyone."

"Es okay, Chole Hart," Ignacio said giving Joel a wink, "Esas cosas puedan ser una maldición."

"That's a big sausage you got there. Looks good," Joel said.

"Ju want asausages, Chole Hart?" He turned and pointed out the butcher's table.

"No, I am meeting a friend for lunch soon."

"Grondsfother!" Ignacio said suddenly. "I waz nameed ofter mi *grondsfother*!"

"Your grandfather," Joel confirmed.

Tom emerged suddenly from the crowd. "Iggy!" he yelled with a big smile and threw his arms around Ignacio.

"Tomás!" Ignacio returned, accepting Tom's embrace.

Tom turned to Joel.

"I was just about to go find you," Joel said.

"Well, looks like I found you first!" Tom extended his hand. "I see that you have met Iggy."

Joel took Tom's hand and shook it, though was a bit jealous that he hadn't warranted a hug. "Yes, we just met right before you got here."

"Deed I got asausages on ju, mi amigo?" Ignacio said to Tom.

"I don't think so," said Tom quickly surveying his shirt. "I'm hungry." Tom looked at Joel. "Sausage?"

"Sausage would be great," Joel answered.

"Then we hab asausages together Tomás an Chole Hart," Ignacio said in celebration.

Tom took his place between the two boys and hung a firm arm over the shoulder of each and together they walked to the butcher's table.

# 21

Joel returned to the Iron Horse. His time with Ignacio and Tom continued to joyfully resonate and color his mood. He would go with Tom in the morning to the canal.

Joel went to his room, but Hart was not there. From all appearances, he hadn't been there for some time. Joel went downstairs and poked around. He was nowhere to be found there either. Joel located Mr. Wrench.

"Mister Wrench," Joel asked in the politest voice he could muster, "do you happen to know where my father, Mister Hart, is?"

"I believe that he accompanied a man to the location where they are building the canals," Mr. Wrench said. "They departed earlier this afternoon. No doubt he will return with the barge before dark."

This was unexpected. Even so, Joel thought, it showed that his father was pulling his weight on this one.

"Thank you, Mister Wrench," Joel said. "While I await the return of my father, may I visit the Iron Horse's reading room?"

"Of course, Master Hart," Mr. Wrench replied.

Joel went to the reading room. It was just off the sitting room, the latter, recall, located to the right as one entered the foyer. The room smelled surprisingly fresh; surprising because it appeared that no one ever spent time in the room. He had expected it to be a bit musty. The bookshelves went from floor to ceiling, Joel estimating the room to be about twelve-feet high. A narrow ladder on wheels was connected to a rail just off the top of the highest shelf, which, he thought, would allow him to venture upwards to see what literary treasures were hiding on the top shelf. It was well known that folks kept the provocative books up there, out of reach of children and newly converted Christians.

Eureka! Just as he had thought. The very first book he spied on the top shelf, once climbing the ladder, of course, was a book authored by Plato—the *Symposium*. He had not heard of this book. By way of his Uncle Yusuf, he had read what philosophers referred to as "the trial and death of Socrates," which was constituted of four dialogues—the *Euthyphro*, *Apology*, *Crito*, and *Phaedo*. He vacillated between preferring the *Crito* and the *Phaedo*. The *Crito* because of Socrates' exchange with "the Law," which, it seemed to Joel, cast Socrates as a kind of proto-capitalist, and the *Phaedo* because it recorded the day of Socrates' execution. In fact, aside from some rather dense ontology, the dialogue was almost entirely about *death*! What young mind wouldn't enjoy that?

Joel removed the book, descended the ladder, and found the most comfortable loveseat in the room. It reminded him of the red fustian velveteen jobber in the portico back home. He opened the book. The first thing noted by the translator was that the ancient Greek word *symposia* meant "drinking-party". This was already a very good omen, Joel thought. The second thing the translator mentioned was that the theme of the dialogue was *love*, beginning with the in-and-outs of *erôs*, which the translator exuberantly cast as *sexual desire*. Another good omen. No doubt this was why the book had been hidden away up on the top shelf! Joel praised his good judgment for having ascended the ladder on his first visit to the reading room.

The dialogue was a bit difficult to follow at first. It begins with Apollodorus on his way to a party, maybe?, in celebration of the playwright Agathon who had just won some big prize. This must be the drinking-party, Joel surmised. Apollodorus, great name, a friend of Socrates', is asked to recount to someone a story that he had already told to Glaucon. About the drinking-party? Wait, Joel thought, isn't Apollodorus heading *to* the drinking-party? Or, had he just been asked to retell the story about heading to a drinking-party? Dammit Plato! The smart thing to do, Joel thought, was to just go with his hunch that Apollodorus was telling the story.

While walking with Socrates to the dinking-party, then, Apollodorus says in his story that Socrates had taken an unexpected detour and ended up standing on some neighbor's porch, frozen like a statue. Okay, Joel thought, the story thus far is this: Apollodorus is retelling some guy a story about heading to a drinking party in celebration of Agathon. Got it! Now, Apollodorus says that while Socrates is frozen on the porch, a guy who knows Socrates pretty well, a guy named Aristodemus, another great name, tells Agathon to just let Socrates be. He will eventually snap out of it and will then come to the party. It's his thing. Does it all the time.

Apollodorus *finally* settles down a few pages into the dialogue and the stage-setting is complete. Good, Joel thought—we are at the party. After dinner a proposal is made to give speeches honoring love. Now we're talking. Phaedrus kicks things off by declaring love to be a great and awesome god. Boring! This goes on much longer than Joel thought was necessary. Love is good. It causes people to sacrifice. "Yeah, yeah," Joel said aloud.

Pausanias was next. His speech begins at marginal number 180c. According to a translator's footnote, which Joel normally ignored, but read in this case, Pausanias is identified as Agathon's *lover*. "Really?" Joel said. His face felt flushed. He was floored just to read it. There it was all matter-of-factly and such. He looked around to find that he was still alone in the reading room. His heart raced. He read the footnote again just to make sure that it had said what he thought it had said. And it said what he thought it had said! Joel could see why the *Symposium* was a top-shelfer. Pausanias, a man, was lover to Agathon, also a man! So, Joel thought, this sort of thing goes all the way back to the ancients—a love between *men*? Why hadn't he heard about this before? His father had joked with him about his giant. Did he know of this sort of thing? If so, he didn't seem judgmental about it. Took it almost matter-of-factly, like the footnote. His Uncle Yusuf didn't seem to mind the story of him and his giant either. Were they more enlightened than Joel had judged? If Plato was writing about it, it must be important. Joel noted to himself that even his goddamned tutors had not ever mentioned this, after forcing him to read *Oedipus* no less! Joel definitely wanted to hear what Pausanias had to say about love—or rather, what Plato writes Apollodorus as having recalled Pausanias saying at the party about love. The juggling of participles was going to be a real challenge, Joel thought. But it looked like it might be worth the effort.

Now, Pausanias says that there are two kinds of love. The first is *Common Love*, which he poetically calls *Common Aphrodite*, the second is *Heavenly Love*, which he calls *Heavenly Aphrodite*. Apparently, these are two distinct goddesses that represent two distinct kinds of love. Which of these, asks Pausanias, should he praise in his speech? Joel's bet was on the latter. It was heavenly after all.

The first, *Common Love*, is expressed as sexual desire. Joel took his bet back—it'd be *great* if Pausanias praised *this* sort of love, even if only a little, before moving to blabbing about the heavenly sort. Pausanias continued—Common Love strives to bring about the natural result of the sexual act. But this sounded boringly biological, Joel thought. He knew of the birds and the bees and this was definitely along those lines. It looks to be aimed at procreating? Pausanias then suggests that this sort of love is the sort expressed by men when they desire women and boys, both of whom are inferior to men. Boys? Okay, back the cart up. Sounds like it may not be connected to reproduction after all. No one thinks they're making babies with boys. Sounds like Pausanias is saying that it is the desire for the sort of *pleasure* one receives in one's being intimate with other *bodies*, whether male or female. Maybe some are attracted just to female bodies, some just to male bodies, some to both, and maybe some to neither? Joel secretly reflected and saw that his desire for Tom was kind of like this. He certainly had no interest in having *children* with Tom. He didn't know if Tom could even read. The intimacy he secretly fantasized about was definitely of the physical kind. It started and stopped with physical shenaniganery. It was simply the heat of it all when he was in Tom's presence.

It felt oddly liberating to openly acknowledge this about himself, even if only *to* himself. It seemed like he was honoring some aspect of his nature that he had always felt needed to be kept secret. But here Plato was just talking all about it in the open.

Then there is *Heavenly Love*. This sort of love has only to do with a love for males. Okay that was unexpected. Maybe Heavenly Love ought to be praised after all. The love can extend to boys, though Pausanias notes that the handsome boys about whom he is talking are not little boys but are much older—old enough to grow facial hair. Joel thought that perhaps it would have been clearer had Pausanias used the term "young man," and not "boy". A translator's mistake? Tom had some peach fuzz on his chin. That surely counted. He fell within the range of those who could be loved in this way. Joel softly rubbed his own chin. It felt a *little* fuzzy. He had gone through "the change," as his mother had once called it. Hart said that technically it was called "puberty". It was times like these when Joel wished that he was Jewish. Take this very scenario. Were he Jewish, he would have had *bar mitzvah*, which would have secured beyond doubt the idea that he was no longer a boy, fuzz or no, not to mention the receiving of some serious cash. But Hart had said that even foregoing said ritual Joel was now a man—a *young* man. So, let the Common or Heavenly Love commence—didn't matter which at this point!

Joel had once heard Hart tell his Uncle Yusuf, who had just turned forty, to cheer up, for Aristotle had said that one becomes an adult man at fifty, the joke being that even at forty he was still not an adult male. Of course, it was probably the case that Uncle Yusuf had been born with a beard. So, there was that. But according to Pausanias, to be attracted to the male, in terms of Heavenly Love, was not really a physical sort of attraction but was instead to find a kind of pleasure in that which is more intelligent. So, that's why women and boys are attracted to men? Men also will be attracted to men—in this case the less intelligent desiring the more intelligent? That sounded right, for it reminded Joel of his experience with his magnificent giant, though for this to be correct, he would have to admit that he was the less intelligent one in the scenario.

If only he could combine his giant's towering intellect with Tom's handsome face and muscular body. *That*, Joel thought, would be an object worth desiring—wouldn't matter what you called it: common or heavenly!

Joel heard Hart's voice. He must have returned from his visit to the canal. Joel plucked a hair from his head and placed it between the pages to mark the place where he had stopped reading, closed the book, quickly mounted the ladder, and inserted the *Symposium* back into its sacred space there on the top shelf. He would return to the book after dinner. He thought it fortunate that Plato had had the wherewithal to write about such things. The *Symposium* was surely proof of Plato's deep affection for humanity. Although he knew it to be untrue, Joel nevertheless felt, as he did with all great works of art, that the book had been written just for him. The thought was comforting.

# 22

Supper was served at six o'clock on the dot. Tonight's menu included pork stew and biscuits slathered in butter. Many patrons simply sunk their biscuit directly into the thick stew. Joel was served a watered-down cup of ale. Since the digging had commenced, the ground water had a rather unpleasant aftertaste, and the kitchen staff found that diluting it with ale made drinking palatable. Even so, about halfway through the rather large cup he found himself feeling warm and loose. Hart was saddled with having to drink the thicker yeasty undiluted concoction. His face was flushed after just one swallow.

"Tell me about your visit to the dock," Hart said. "Did you learn anything?"

"I learned that one can get seriously killed," Joel replied.

"Killed you say? In what manner?"

"You know, crushed by falling crates or cut in half by snapping ropes," Joel said.

"Aside from how easy it is to be killed on the dock, did you learn anything about whether our company utilizes the warehouse or stockyard?"

"I learned something about bulks," Joel said.

"Bulks."

"Yes, there are different categories of bulks—break bulks, neo bulks, liquid bulks."

"Are any of those bulks related to our company?"

"Don't know. Didn't get that far," Joel said. "What about you? I was surprised to learn that you had ventured out to see the canal."

"Your man Tom was right—the pit they have dug could swallow most of Lion Street, buildings and all!"

Joel enjoyed hearing Hart refer to Tom as "your man."

"Did anything you observe inspire a plan to muck up their project?" Joel asked.

"No, not really," Hart answered, "But I was struck by the number of workers who claimed that during the digging some rather valuable treasures had been unearthed."

"Treasures?" Joel asked. "Like what?"

"Apparently several small chests filled with jewelry, though most contained rancid perfumes or hosiery or someone's private notebooks. Many boys reported that they continue to unearth silver Dutch coins and such." Hart paused and then said, "I overheard a manager complain that several on his team were no longer showing to work. They are apparently spending their time digging for treasure. The locals are obsessed, he said. They come to the canal at night when workers have gone home and sift through the spoils."

Someone from the waitstaff made rounds to see if anyone wanted more. Hart told them that he and the boy were fine.

"Oh, I did see *something* that I thought would interest you," Hart said.

"Oh yeah?" Joel replied with a pretense of boredom.

"I was walking near the privies when I saw your Mister Gouverneur Morris!" Hart said.

Joel's jaw dropped.

"I know, right?" said Hart.

"*The* Gouverneur Morris? The one my glorious giant...?"

"One and the same," Hart replied. "I mean, how many men would have had the bad luck of being baptized with such a hideous name? Good looking fellow. You'll appreciate him," Hart said. "The pegleg does make him interesting to the eye. I didn't linger to eavesdrop into his conversation, however, for he was talking with a rather scary fellow."

"Scary, how so?"

"He appeared to be an Indian fellow, dark skinned, lean, easily as tall as your glorious giant. Long black hair. He wore a tight black suit, buttoned up to his neck, long boots, and a wide-brimmed black hat. His face was scared with ferocious looking tattoos, which accented his high-cheek bones and narrow eyes. His irises were pitch black. I had only seen drawings of this sort of thing in books—the face tattoos, I mean."

"That *is* scary," Joel said.

"I asked Mister King, the man who took me to the canal, about the two men and he says that that man is Mister Morris' *henchman*. Says he's an Algonquin warrior. Mister Morris, who, according to Mister King, apparently lingers around the privy area, hired the warrior as a kind of mercenary to handle the local Mohicans. Mister King assured me that rumor has it that the henchman has also been used by Mister Morris to dispose of stubborn landowners and local businessmen who have tried to halt the canal project. People report that men disappear into the privy never to return."

"Henchman—like *assassin*?" Joel asked

"Like assassin," Hart repeated. "We need to proceed very carefully. He may be more dangerous to us than falling crates and snapping ropes."

# 23

After dinner Hart went upstairs to the room and Joel returned to the reading room. He climbed the ladder and took the *Symposium* from the shelf. He descended the ladder and sat on the same loveseat as before. He opened the book but found no hair. Had someone been reading the book during dinner?

The story had had a great enough impact that Joel really didn't need the hair. He knew *exactly* where he had left off—with Pausanias.

He quickly found the passage in which Pausanias begins speaking about Heavenly Love. This, recall, is a love that desires one's *mind*, and in particular one's *intelligence*. Pausanias says that this sort of love is related to the god Uranus, and consequently it only speaks to the love of *males*. Not sure why that follows, Joel thought. The idea was maybe this: males have superior intellects, and if one is drawn to intelligence, then one will be drawn to males.

Boys, of course, are young males who have yet to develop their intellect. That needs to be done by way of the guidance of an older male whose intellect is fully realized. The younger man is attracted to the older man for what he can offer, and the older to the younger man for what he can potentially offer—a lifetime of companionship! But in the interim, the older man can enjoy the pleasures of the younger man's physical beauty. Very capitalist really. *Quid pro quo.* This for that. So long as no one is coerced, nothing wrong with the trade. The trade, Joel saw in his mind, would be sex for education. Would be anti-capitalist to demand that the teacher teach for free. Even so, the aim of the investment of the energy of both parties was to produce a lifelong companionship. In the *Symposium*, Pausanias was probably the younger and Agathon the playwright the older. Was the giant Joel's Agathon?

Men who desired young men but only set out to exploit them for sexual favors would be doing something vicious, says Pausanias. In fact, laws should be enacted that prohibited such exploitation. Yes, Joel thought, in a free market you must nevertheless make laws to protect against fraud and exploitation—though the potential conflict here was that the imposition of laws might upset the idea of the market's being *free*. Actors in the market should seek to improve only themselves. According to Adam Smith, these self-interested actions would convert selfish action into a good for the entire community. Pausanias says when lovers act so as to satisfy their own self-interest—the young man pursues knowledge the older man sex—this ultimately can produce a good for both. Love and business are truly alike, Joel thought.

So why make laws against exploitation? Wouldn't the young man who had been duped by the older learn a valuable lesson? That's worth something. Besides, as Smith suggests, in a truly free market we wouldn't need laws. The way a bad actor is punished in a free market, a market without laws, is to no longer do business with that actor. This would be enough to get potential bad actors from acting badly. Act badly, no one enters contracts with you anymore. But if by being exploited one learns a valuable lesson, and the young man's self-interested aim is to acquire knowledge, then what's the problem? We should all be exploited at least once. This was all making sense, Joel thought. It eased any guilt he had in knowing that he was exploiting the good Mr. Carmichael and the innocent shareholders of the navigation company. Pausanias says that *virtue* should be the ultimate end that each lover pursues. Joel wasn't sure about all this talk about virtue, but to get sex and offer nothing of value in return was certainly a breach of capitalist principles. Offering someone in return for sex a lesson about exploitation is not *nothing*. It is definitely something. So, Pausanias seemed wrong about our needing laws, Joel thought.

The large clock in the foyer struck eight bells. This was followed almost immediately by the sounding of the clock standing at the end of the hall on the second floor, which was followed by a clock located somewhere in the back kitchen. It was almost time to return to the room. He began to thumb through the pages. Something caught his eye at around marginal mark 189c.

Aristophanes, the famous playwright—a lot of playwrights at this goddammed party, Joel thought—offered his speech in the form of a mythical story. He told of a time long ago when human beings were different than they are now. Humans were originally in the form of strange couplets, like conjoined twins or something—two heads, two torsos, two sets of genitalia, four arms, four legs, and so on. There were three types of conjoined-being: Male-Male, Female-Female, and Male-Female. Joel could just picture it. Even so, he could barely stand the company of Hart. What must it have been like to have someone always in your face day in and day out, attached to you at your abdomen no less?

According to Aristophanes, these human beings made the gods' lives absolutely miserable. To put an end to the misery-making, Zeus cut each couplet in half, severing the conjoined twins one from the other. Apollo, who sounds like a real douche in the story, forced them to gaze upon their gashes! How horrible, Joel thought. He could see it now. Apollo then tied the wound, which is now one's bellybutton. Huh, so that's how they got there. But this wasn't the end of it. The newly halved saps where all mixed together, like cards shuffled in a deck, which set each half in a lifelong search of his or her natural partner. This, Joel realized, explained why some men seek men, some women seek women, and some men seek women, or some women seek men. How sad that the gods had done this to us. But it explained why Hart sought a woman, and why he seeks a man. They must come from different lines of the original humans, Hart from the Male-Female line and Joel from the Male-Male line. Of course, Hart, at least according to Pausanias, should desire a man, at the very least for his superior intellect. But perhaps the missing partner had a greater pull on him than a highly intelligent man. The outlier was Uncle Yusuf, for he did not seek anyone—but then the story about Misses Tontine's midnight laundry services came to mind. Perhaps he sought women? Though it had to be admitted that Misses Tontine looked like a man wearing women's clothes, so who knows who Uncle Yusuf desired?—the thought about Misses Tontine being a man wearing women's clothes was a surprisingly erotic thought, and Joel let it linger.

"Thank you very much," Joel heard Hart say from the other room. "In here, you say?"

"Just through there, yes," said a stranger's voice.

Joel quickly climbed the ladder and put the *Symposium* back on the top shelf. Hart entered the reading room before Joel could descend. He almost jumped, but it seemed too dangerous.

"There you are," Hart said. "I got to thinking that maybe the library had a book about the local Indian tribes." He ignored Joel who still stood on the ladder and began looking up and down and across shelves left and right. "I would like to see if there is anything on the meaning of those facial tattoos."

Joel began to look over the top shelf as though helping Hart out.

"Look here!" Hart said excitedly. He bent over and removed a book from a lower shelf. He opened it up to inspect its pages. "As I had hoped, there are some drawings of several men and women in their tribal dress."

"Any tattoos?" Joel asked, working himself down the ladder.

Hart flit through quite a few pages with his thumb. "Here are some drawings of facial tattoos," he said. "But they don't look like those on our hencher's face." He looked some more. "Nothing here about the meaning of the tattoos."

The foyer clock struck one bell. It must now be eight-fifteen.

"We should get to bed," Hart said. "We have a lot to do tomorrow. You are still going with Tom to the canal, yes?"

"Yes," Joel confirmed. "What are you going to do?"

"I will go down to the docks and see if I can't pick up where you left off," Hart said.

"Be mindful of the crates and ropes," Joel cautioned.

"Be mindful of Mister Morris and his assassin," Hart said as he returned the book to its shelf. "Maybe just avoid the privies altogether."

# 24

Tom met Joel in the foyer of the Iron Horse. The clocks in their off-kilter way had just sounded seven bells each. It was a clear and warm Saturday morning. Mr. Wrench had instructed staff to open the windows, which allowed the fragrance of the grasses to softly visit every corner and crack inside the place.

The kitchen staff set aside a plate of biscuits and sausage gravy for the boys to share. They also shared a cup of strong coffee. They ate at a large table back in the kitchen, for Mr. Wrench had forbidden Tom from eating in the dining room with guests.

After breakfast they made their way to the dock and boarded the barge. It was long and flat, the deck about five feet above the water. No rails. There was a massive iron furnace with a tall smokestack installed at the boat's stern, which powered a large paddlewheel. Large crates had been placed at the bow to balance the thing out. On the black iron boiler was painted FITCH in bold gold letters. It was designed specifically to move supplies upriver for the Western Inland Lock Navigation Company. Fancier versions of the powered boat were said to be working up and down the Delaware River. The men called it a *steamboat*. In addition to carrying several tons of beams and iron rods, it had room for about fifty men. Several chickens had made their way onboard and now strutted about the deck. Tom and Joel would disembark when the boat reached Van Schaick Island, about ten miles upriver from Albany.

As the barge moved slowly up the Hudson, the deck hypnotically rose and fell. Every seven minutes or so two very muscular men would shovel coal into the furnace, which released a thick column of black smoke out the top of the stack. The thing puffed and pounded and shook the entire boat. Water was pumped from the river below into the boiler by several men working a large wooden handle. The furnace boiled the water, and the steam was diverted out the boiler through a large steel pipe. A lever-handle stood at the ready to control the amount of steam that was released hissing angrily into the mechanism that churned the large wheel. Tom had been told by a boatswain on a previous ride upriver that that was the *engine*. About twenty minutes into their journey the captain told everyone that if something went wrong with the power system, they would hear a loud whistle. He turned and waived his arm signaling an engineer to pull a rope at which time a loud steam whistle let loose. It could be heard echoing up and down the river for at least half a minute. Once sounded they were to jump ship and try to make their way to shore. Joel realized that for this plan to work, one would have to know how to swim.

Tom turned to Joel, "I don't know how to swim, do you?"

"No, I do not." Joel replied.

Tom pointed out to Joel the Minister John Bassett of the local Dutch Reform Church. He was wearing his ministerial apparel, and appeared to be standing uncomfortably next to a black slave who had a heavy bag of potatoes slung over his shoulder and another at his feet. Joel had not noticed either when boarding.

"Why does he stand like that, I wonder?" Joel asked.

"The minister? He is standing a sort of guard. Travels on the barge whenever a company slave is transported," Tom answered. "They've lost several to men having thrown them from the barge into the Hudson. The company pays Minister Bassett to accompany them."

"Thrown into the river?" Joel asked.

"Into the river," Tom answered.

A man who had overheard Tom added, "Today the good Minister is heading upriver to bury several of those savages who were kilt yesterday in the pit. That's why he's really here. Their bodies are up there stinkin' up the place. He should've gone up there yesterday. I think that that one with the potatoes there is the brother to one of 'em. Should throw him into the river so he can join 'em in the hereafter."

The Minister had surely overheard the account just given, for the eavesdropper had said everything loud enough for most passengers on the barge to hear. The Minister looked at Joel and cleared his throat and took a few steps away from the man he was "protecting" and then looked down at his feet.

\*\*\*

As they began to reach the southern tip of Van Schaick Island, where the Mohawk flows into the Hudson, the barge began a slow zigzag starboard, the aim appearing to maneuver the barge to steer it into the Mohawk River, the latter port side. The captain overshot the Mohawk and continued almost a half mile up the Hudson, continuing all the while to veer starboard. The captain yelled out something and the barge began to turn to the left. Its long starboard side now exposed perpendicular to the heavy current of the Hudson, the barge was pushed back downriver, while at the same time heading toward the island. The deck pitched noticeably, men having to steady themselves. The chickens hemmed and hawed and sought higher ground moving to the tops of the large crates at the bow. The barge was being pushed back toward the southern end of the island, where the Mohawk empties into the Hudson, where they had been about ten minutes ago. The barge looked to be aimed at penetrating the place where the Mohawk opened into the Hudson. The current of the Mohawk now began to push against the bow, the barge slowing considerably in its forward direction. The barge now looked to be at the mercy of the powerful currents of both the Hudson and Mohawk. The captain shouted, "Full steam!" The muscular men shoveled coal, the valve operator set the steam at full blast into the engine. The speed of the paddlewheel's rotation increased.

Before the power of both rivers could run the barge aground, or perhaps worse, capsize the thing, which seemed more likely to Joel, the barge had moved out of the grips of the Hudson, the pitch of the deck returning level, and was now heading squarely up the Mohawk.

Off starboard they could now see the inland western side of the island. To their left was the North American continent. The hypnotic rise and fall of the deck returned.

The wharf at Van Schaick Island was busy. It looked very much like any port, really, though it was occupied by what appeared to be an army of black men engaged in hard physical labor. Men on top of men. Men with no smiles and grimaced faces. Their appendages moved more like those of automatons than human beings. Many were shirtless. Clothing and bare skin alike were eerily covered in grey. The dust from the great pit seemed to be the cause. It covered the entire wharf and adjacent buildings. Men with long sticks on horseback moved back and forth among the laborers. He now noticed many white laborers also in grey clothes whose hair had also been greyed by the same dust. The men looked to be fettered with shackles and chains.

Tom said that those chained men were prisoners from the State Prison who the Governor had lent to the Western Inland Lock Navigation Company. He was told to stay clear of them. The black men were enslaved men brought up from Virginia. They were "Company" property. Although they were not wearing chains, the institution of slavery had bound these men with its own chains—ungodly yet omnipotent, whose chains were invisible and yet stronger than the iron shackles that bound the state prisoners. The invisibility of the fetters made ignoring slavery easier for a nation of pathologically self-ignorant Christians. In witnessing in person such absolute control over men, Joel felt what theologians refer to as demonic dread, the kind of dread one feels when walking through a graveyard even in broad daylight—ominous and otherworldly, the safety of the sunlight an illusion. The dead that haunt the graveyard haunt it just as much by day as by night! And it is infinitely more terrifying to encounter such realities in the light of day, for then it will be made clear to you that *nothing* is safe.

Joel turned and discovered the man with the potato bags standing only a few feet away. He found it difficult to refer to the man as a *slave*. To utter the word was to admit to his own complicity in the reality of it. But he knew full well that there was a difference between this man and those prisoners of the state. Those men had deserved their punishment. The good Minister was no longer at his side but was off laughing with several members of the crew. Joel had never been so physically close to a slave! There, he said it. Unlike those on the island, this man was not covered in grey dust. His clothes were heavy, too heavy for the heat of the day. Joel now noticed that he was barefoot. He smelled like any man he had ever smelled. Joel looked at the man, though was ashamed to look directly into his face. But he peeked. The man's eyes whose whites were yellowed were profoundly still, yet powerful, heavily sunk into his skull. Suddenly they turned to Joel. Each man recognized the other; they allowed each other entry and found their common humanity. A smile. Men were present. Joel could see *him*, and he Joel. The man looked back over the Mohawk to those on the wharf. Even so, Joel continued to feel the man there. He again felt shame, this time for feeling grateful that he was not this man, that he was none of those grey covered men. But Joel *was* this man. The man he encountered was not some "other" but was of his own kind. The man Joel saw was not in the eyes. He inhabited the "space" that Joel inhabited, that Tom, Hart, Frances, his giant inhabited, and that Mr. Wrench inhabited—the "space" in which *all* men and *only* men exist. No other kind of thing exists in this space. The man and Joel had met in that place *eternal*. Joel thought of Pausanias' praise of heavenly love.

The capitalist, Joel reminded himself in trying to rebuild the dike, *must* own materials and labor. But the reminder didn't help. The anxiety did not relent. Men *were* labor! The anxiety grew more potent. The posted papers he saw on the warehouse's wall when they arrived, which he found almost comical when he first read them, now, in light of the terrifying spectacle on display, and his encounter with the *man* enslaved, had transfigured into gratuitous wicked stories that formed the plot of some badly written tragedy. It was like that optical illusion which at one moment appears to be a rabbit, at another a duck. The change is a change in perspective, in point of view, not fact. Nothing of the drawing changes, and yet in the wink of an eye *everything* changes! The Kingdom of Heaven is on earth, but men do not see it. Joel was Saul on the road to Damascus. His encounter with this man enslaved on the Mohawk was Saul's encounter with Christ risen.

Was it possible that the anxiety, which had become an uncomfortable dread, had as its origin in Joel's adoption of capitalistic ideology? The ideology that thinks of human beings as nothing more than *property*, as things to be *owned*? Was his seeing the host of grey men simply the occasion for this dread's unwanted appearance? The theory failed to align with reality—with humanity. The yellowed eyed man was not the sort of being that *could* be owned. He wasn't anywhere to be found in his body, no more than the beauty of a symphony of Mozart was to be found in the agitation of the air! And yet it was *through* the eyes that Joel was able to encounter the man—it was through the agitation of the air that one encounters the beauty of Mozart.

Slave labor, in fact any form of labor cast in the light of capitalism, seen from this new point of view, Joel thought, was nothing less than *contempt* for man. As Saul had been forced to change his name to Paul, no longer identifying with his previous self, Joel realized that he could no longer call himself "The Capitalist". It was a silly name anyway. A child's name. It was the name of someone who had gotten used to the smell of rotten things such as slavery and self-righteous Christian hypocrisy. But now such things wreaked, and nothing had ever smelled as rancid to Joel as these things did now. Perhaps the evilest man on that barge was the good Minister, for if anyone knew that slavery was evil, it was him. And yet, he does nothing. He is paid to protect the Company's property. Perhaps the fault lay with his master? Joel could not recall reading a single sacred passage in which Jesus had denounced slavery.

This change in perspective, in paradigm, was sudden and unexpected. Rabbit to duck indeed. Joel wanted to return to Hart and together return to Uncle Yusuf and to their duplex in the lower eastside of New York City. He wished that there was never a Western Inland Navigation Lock Company. He wanted to wash off the stink that his historical times had covered him in. But he knew that the stink would never wash off. He wanted Ignacio and Tom and the man with the smiling yellow eyes to come home with him. He missed his mother, Frances. What on earth had happened? All he wanted to do was spend the day with Tom and do a little spying. And now he's Saint Paul. Sheesh!

The engineer disengaged the paddlewheel, which almost immediately stopped turning, and pulled another large lever that through a system of turning thick clocklike gears elevated the wheel out of the water. He then turned the valve-lever that was fastened to the steel pipe that exited the boiler and a violent shot of steam popped and hissed from the open valve. The air-pressure noticeably changed. The captain steered the now coasting barge toward a man who stood on the dock. "Yur good, keep a cumin," he yelled to the captain. The natural flow of the river, which ran against the boat's heading, served as the barge's braking system. At first Joel had wondered whether they were coming in too fast. But clearly the captain and crew knew what they were doing, for the barge was steered right along the dock coming to a stop almost precisely where the man on the dock was standing. Several crew members jumped from the deck of the barge to the dock while others cast large ropes from the barge onto the dock. "Secure the bow," yelled the captain. The man on the dock nearest the bow quickly tethered the rope to a dock cleat, where the second man along with the man awaiting the barge pulled their rope to bring the stern of the barge alongside the dock. "Secure the stern," yelled the captain, and the two men tied the rope to a dock cleat.

The barge was now officially moored—something that Joel could no longer say about his own life.

# 25

The island was not where the real work was being done. From the dock they boarded a large canoe which took them directly across the Mohawk to the mainland, to the small town called Cohoes. There were two smaller barges that were in operation that took supplies across. Men populated those too. But there was a rather large wait, and so most men took the large canoes. Once they reached the mainland, they walked the right side of a wide, graveled road toward the site along with several hundred men. An equal number of dead faced men who had finished their workday were walking the left side of the road back toward the town. Joel thought this must be what it was like to be in a war.

The canal was large indeed, though not as impressive as Joel had imagined. It lay some distance to the west of the Mohawk and ran parallel. The design, Joel surmised, was to allow a small vessel heading upriver to enter this canal, which would be filled with water, the vessel would be floated upriver, and then would reenter the Mohawk. If it needed to get further upriver, it could remain in the canal and exit when it arrived at its destination. Vessels returning to the Hudson would simply float down the Mohawk with the natural current. The wall closest to the river had already been built with wooden and iron beams and was now being bricked bottom to top. Scaffolding supported more than a hundred men, and even more mixing the mortar and hoisting platforms of stacked bricks from the ground up to the masons.

"It's not as big as I expected," Joel said.

"No? Come with me," insisted Tom.

The two walked to the edge of the pit and Tom pointed to a wooden staircase that would allow them to descend into the great hole. As they made their way down the stairs, the pit's walls began to swallow them up. Once at the bottom, Joel felt the magnitude of the depth, width, and length of the canal.

"Okay, I take it back," Joel said, "It's really big."

It was true that the entirety of Lion Street, buildings and all, could fit into the canal. Joel could easily picture it.

"Told you," Tom said.

They stood against the wall and took it all in.

"I need to get to the materials depot," Tom said.

"Materials depot?"

"It's like a huge makeshift stockyard," Tom answered. "We keep track of all the supplies. Right up my alley."

"Yes, that makes sense," Joel said. "Do I go with you or ..."

"No, best not. They barely tolerate me, and I work there. Hang out here, and you can gather the information you need for your project, and when you're ready, just follow the flow of returning men down that road we walked, take a canoe back to the island. The last barge departs to Albany at five. You may have to squeeze onboard. Many of the men will be drunk, so be mindful not to upset anyone. Don't want to get thrown overboard."

"Are you serious?"

"Well, they won't throw you overboard, but they will entertain themselves by scaring you into thinking that they will. If you miss the last barge, or if it's full and you cannot board, you can take the road that follows along the river back to Albany. It's a ten-mile walk. I've had to do that most nights after I am finished here. There are always plenty of supply carts heading south for you to hitch a ride on."

"I can wait for you," Joel said.

"I probably won't be let go until late tonight. I've been staying the night in the depot along with several others. As you can see, there are so many men moving about, we probably wouldn't find one another anyway."

"I'm sure you're right. But I had not thought this through."

"You'll be fine," Tom said. "Until we meet again on Monday, then?"

"Yes, I'll come by the warehouse on Monday," Joel confirmed.

Tom quickly disappeared into the worksite.

Joel took a deep breath and reminded himself why he was there. But his plans had changed since his experience of the enslaved men and his encounter with the man on the barge. Instead of ruining the company, the aim would be to figure out a way to only screw things up enough to *temporarily* lower the stock price. Nobody needed to get hurt. We were talking stock prices, not people. Of course, the stocks were owned by people, but if he employed his genius right, perhaps he could get the stock price to dip just long enough to cover the time that he and Hart had to pay Mr. Carmichael back, where after that time things could recover, and the prices would go up again and the investors would not be harmed. Even Mr. Carmichael would be happy. All parties would be concerned *temporarily* but not harmed. The trick will be to figure out how to make all this mayhem temporary.

His interest in speaking with Mister Morris was relit, if only to get for his giant an answer to whether he was in on the thing with Stupid Johnny, but he did not want to draw any attention from Mr. Morris' hencher. Joel thought that were he to throw enough sand into the gears here, enough to slow things down, he might even bring about a lull that lasted long enough to give Tom and his yellowed-eyed acquaintance from the barge some much deserved downtime. He added this to his list of reasons to temporarily sink the Western Inland Navigation Lock Company stock price. He was feeling back to his usual self, though he was serious about rethinking the whole capitalism thing.

# 26

There was a rather large area in the camp set aside for water. Hanging from the rims of the troughs were perhaps a hundred ladles. The troughs set aside for the black laborers did not have ladles. They had to use their hands. The water levels were also noticeably lower. Many of the white laborers took long swigs, swallowed only some of the water, swished what remained around in their mouths, and spit it out into the troughs set aside for the black laborers. They would then recompose themselves and politely rehang the ladle for the next man.

Joel approached one of the troughs designated for white laborers, took a ladle, dipped it in, and drank all of it. No one seemed to even notice him, so he placed the ladle on a rim of one of the troughs designated for black men. His shame returned, this time for feeling fortunate that he could drink from the trough with a ladle, whose water wasn't poisoned with the spit of other men. And like the good minister, Joel knew that he too had lacked the courage to do anything to remedy it. Putting the ladle where he did while no one noticed was the most courageous act he could summon? He had always thought of himself as better than this.

After he left the area his critical self-reflection faded—but only slightly—and the thought that everything was going to be okay was possible again.

No one Joel had encountered knew who Gouverneur Morris was, though many did admit to seeing a man with a pegleg in the camp. And no one knew him to oversee anything. All had confidently claimed that the man in charge of this project was in fact a Mr. Philip Schuyler. What they did know, which confirmed something that Hart had noted at dinner, is how treasure hunting was infinitely more enjoyable than digging the canal. Before heading back to the canoes, Joel thought that he would make a visit to the privies.

Lo and behold there was the assassin! He was talking to a man equally tall and dressed rather elegantly. That *had* to be Morris! No one would be so sillily overdressed in this heat. And, of course, there was the dead giveaway of the missing leg. It was most odd that this location was precisely where Hart said he had run across the two men. Did they have a thing for privies?

Several men exited from the small outhouse next to which Morris and his hencher were standing. Seven in all! How on earth did they fit into such a small space? There were plenty of outhouses. But wait! Several more men now exited the same outhouse! Maybe eight? Yes, Joel counted them: fifteen had exited that outhouse? Impossible! Hart has said the reports were that men go in but never come out. Here, Joel saw no one go in, and yet fifteen came out. The conspiracy of privy-goers spoke with one another for a few minutes and then three went with the hencher and the rest accompanied who Joel had identified as Morris. And yet *another* man emerged from the outhouse and then appeared to stand guard at the outhouse's narrow door. He began surveying the area before him. Joel knew that he would stand out to the man were he to continue to stare. Joel put his head down and walked straight to one of the outhouses. Once inside, as he had thought it was big enough for a single man, two at most. Sixteen was impossible. Joel finished his business and headed back to the canoes. What had he witnessed? He was excited to tell Hart all about it.

# 27

The last barge back to Albany was, as Tom had predicted, full and would not accommodate any more men. Those who wished to return to Albany would have to travel south on the road that ran parallel to the Hudson. Fortunately, word of the barge's fullness had reached Joel while still on the mainland. Before heading back, he would locate the materials depot and find Tom. Perhaps Tom would be up for walking back with him to Albany.

After some effort, Joel found the materials depot, but no one who worked the yard knew of anyone named Tom or anyone who answered to Joel's description of him. This was indeed perplexing. Perhaps Joel had misunderstood what Tom had told him. But he was pretty sure that Tom had said that he worked at the materials depot.

Joel made his way to the road that Tom had told him about. At least he had not misunderstood Tom about that. The road was there. A large sign clearly had ALBANY painted on it with an arrow pointing the way. He saw several flatbeds pulled by horses heading south, and even more in the way of smaller carriages and single riders.

Joel asked around and struck gold—he found a coachman willing to let him ride on one of the running boards. He offered the coachman a nickel, but the man wouldn't take it. Said it wouldn't be Christian of him. Joel was told that when the carriage had reached the town square the coachman would slow the carriage down at which time Joel could jump off. The carriage looked like it could seat about six large men comfortably inside, maybe four Uncle Yusufs. It was a closed gentleman's carriage. Those inside would be relatively protected from the elements. Joel would have to stand on the running board of course and hold on for dear life, especially in the event the horses were brought to anything faster than a working trot. No doubt he would be covered with debris when this was all over. He would ask Mr. Wrench about how one might go about washing one's clothes while staying under the roof of the Iron Horse.

One of the carriage's windows was directly above Joel's head. He was not tall enough to peep in, but he could hear almost everything that was being said. There appeared to be three passengers. A particular part of their conversation caught his attention.

"Morris is looking well these days," said one of the men.

"I hear he just returned from France," said another.

"The Revolution has definitely made living there difficult," said a third.

"Johnson tells me that Morris was almost hung by a mob there," said the second man.

"Really?"

"Yes. The story goes that a mob had surrounded his carriage, in which he and a lover were riding, and he exited the carriage, bent over, and pulled off the leg and swung it around over his head, shouting '*Vive la révolution*!' The mob loved it, applauded, and let the carriage go on its way."

"Amazing that. He certainly has had good fortune. No doubt the woman inside the carriage was another's wife," said the third man.

"You know that that's how he lost the leg?" said the second.

"I did hear something along those lines," said the first.

"Do tell," said the third man.

"Well, he was with the wife of a very powerful man, I won't repeat his name, and the husband walked in on Morris noodling his wife in their bed. He immediately jumped up, still naked mind you, grabbed what he could of his clothes, and fled the bedroom out the window. He was run over by a carriage crossing in front of the house, and eventually lost the leg," said the first man.

"Do tell," repeated the third man, though this time with decadent approval.

"I bet that his whoring around has increased considerably after getting that pegleg," said the second man.

"It *is* very sexy, in a piratesque sort of way," said the third.

"What on earth is he doing *here*?" asked the second man. "I heard that he had plans on running for the Senate."

"I heard that also," said the first.

"I too had heard that also," said the third. "A pirate Senator. How sexy. How butch and sexy."

"I wonder if he takes the leg off when engaged in coitus?" mused the first man.

"I would have him leave it on, if I am being honest," said the second.

"Do tell," said the third with even greater decadent approval than before.

"Scuttlebutt is that he has been hired by the lock company to remove some discovered stash of gold bullion that the British hid during the revolution. Apparently, the Brits just left it here, probably intending to return in secret to retrieve it. Its whereabouts had been discovered last year sometime by a local."

"Who was that I wonder?," asked the second man.

"Dunno. I suspect that the poor sap no longer walks the earth. Morris and his cronies acquired the location's whereabouts and the dig began toot sweet. But everyone got wind of the thing, including the Brits, and pretty soon retrieving the gold was a dangerous proposition. Certain state and private actors concocted the idea of a canal, commandeered the land through eminent domain, which then kept treasure-seekers, especially the Brits, off the land. To help quell any discord, the Western Inland Navigation Lock Company was created and then 'hired' to construct the lock system. They hired many to keep the locals happy, but, of course, there weren't nearly enough men here to do the work."

"The work of making a fake canal?"

"No, the work of locating the bullion," asserted the first man. "Have you not been listening?"

"But I thought that you said that the location had been discovered. Why would you need so many men spread out over such a large area and dig such a ridiculously large hole in the ground?"

"Well, turned out, at least as the thing has been told to me, that the man who had claimed to have located it was lying all along. What it looked like he was doing was recruiting investors to fund the dig. Investors would receive a portion of the bullion treasure once unearthed. At some point the jig would have been up, of course, since the man had only been lying about knowing the treasure's whereabouts, but he would have been long gone with their money before the dance ended. Ironically for him, it looks like his scheme only led to his 'disappearance' once the powers that be heard about his declaring that he knew of the treasure's location."

"His lie also led to Morris' disappointment I imagine."

"To that too. Anyhow, the Governor and Mister Schuyler were able to recruit a slaver out of Virginia, the Governor, and the head of prisons here in New York to provide the needed manpower. The Governor and the head of prisons are expecting to be cut in I imagine. Not sure about the slaver."

"So, you think that that monstrous hole out there is not really the result of pretending to dig a canal, but is in fact the result of failed attempts to find the bullion?"

"Yes, that is what I think."

"I would figure that if it's a lot of bullion, the Brits will likely do whatever they can to retrieve the treasure. Could get ugly for Morris and the others."

"Yes, I wouldn't want to be in their shoes once they recover the gold."

"So," the second man summarized, "the canal project is simply a cover for the extraction of the gold bullion."

"Must be a substantial stash to warrant proposing to build a canal to cover it up," said the second.

"I wonder whether they have found it," said the third man. "I've not seen any sign of it. You would think that there would be such excitement."

"The entire thing is hush hush," said the first. "When they do discover it, my guess is that many who are currently involved in the scheme will also be *disappeared*, if you know what I mean."

"Unsettling to see so many slaves in one place north of the Mason-Dixon," said the third.

"Stanger still to see so many with Morris' *approval*," said the second.

"What do you mean?" asked the third man.

"Morris was among the most vocal at the Continental Congress against the continuing of slavery in the new nation."

"Really? I had not heard that."

"Well, that sounds more noble when said like that," said the second man.

"What do you mean?"

"It wasn't that he was opposed to slavery for *moral* reasons. At least that's not how I understood his view. He simply did not like the idea that southern states could count slaves when putting forward their numbers when seeking representation in Congress but in turn not require slaves to pay taxes. If southerners wanted slaves to count toward the number of Congressional Representatives they would be allotted, they would have to pay a tax on each slave. You can see that he turned the thing around—you know, instead of no taxation without representation, Morris was saying no representation without taxation. Quite a capitalistic move if you ask me," said the second.

"I heard that in several speeches before the Congress he did make *moral* arguments against slavery," said the first man.

"Maybe you are correct," said the second.

"You know that he is referred to as the *penman* of the *Constitution*," said the first man.

"Penman?"

"You know, he penned the document," said the first man while miming writing with a pen.

"Yes, of course, how stupid of me," said the third man.

"But I hear that his views have changed since then," said the second man.

"I have heard that also," said the first. "In fact, the last I also heard, he had proposed New York's seceding from the union."

"And why on earth would he propose that?" asked the third man.

"Dunno," said the second.

"I recently read somewhere that he thought that the nation should entice our best men to run for public office by appealing to their natural greed and pursuit of glory, giving them power to rule. This way their greed will be satisfied in a civil manner and not by way of the sword."

"Now *that* sounds like a capitalistic move," said the second man. He paused then added, "I hear that there is sabotage afoot in the camp."

"I too have heard that also," said the first.

Joel almost lost his footing. His breathing became faster and shallower. Don't fall off! he thought to himself.

"Yes, some man and his son have come up from New York City. They appear to be bent on mucking things up here so as to plummet the price of the company's script," said the second man. "The trouble is that such plummeting would draw attention to the project, which would jeopardize Morris' mission."

"I hear that the son is actually a daughter only disguised as a son. I hear that she is breathtaking."

"I have not seen the couple, so I cannot say. But I would like to see this breathtaking daughter of which you speak."

"Perhaps the son just wants people to *think* that he's a breathtaking daughter dressed up as a son. You know, as part of the ruse? Maybe he's a breathtaking son! Either way, the company's agents have identified them, and I hear that they are currently engaged in plans to thwart their efforts."

"I hear that Morris' men are also engaged in that effort," said the second.

"I too had heard that also," said the first.

# 28

Joel could see the lanterns of the town square. The coachman drove the carriage through the square and commanded the horses to slow to a brief walk. Joel knew that this was his cue to jump from the running board. He jumped knowing that he would have to run some of the landing to keep from stumbling forward onto his face.

By the time he recovered, the carriage had resumed its course and was lost to the night. Joel turned to the town and headed up Lion Street to the Iron Horse.

A small crowd stood on the Iron Horse's porch, on the short, bricked walk, and on the street outside the tavern. As he approached, he heard a woman's voice say, "I believe that that is the boy."

Several men approached him, one placing his large hand on Joel's shoulder. What was this all about?

He heard a man up on the porch yell out, "Mister Wrench, we have found the boy, he is out here." He heard Mr. Wrench from inside the foyer of the Iron Horse say, "Thank the gods! Bring him inside."

The man on the porch turned to the crowd on the street, "Bring the boy here."

The man with his hand on Joel's shoulder leaned in and softly said to Joel, "Son, let's go inside."

Joel was ushered through the crowd, up to the porch, and into the Iron Horse.

"Thank the gods you are safe!" said Mr. Wrench. "We thought that you had been taken."

"Taken?" asked Joel.

"Murdered!" said a man in the foyer.

"Murdered?" Joel mouthed. He recovered his wits. "Where is my father?"

The men began looking at one another with *very* serious looks.

"We are not sure, young man," said a uniformed man.

"Murdered in all likelihood," said a man in the foyer.

"Well, no, no, we do not *know* that," said Mr. Wrench.

"What happened?" Joel asked, tears beginning to involuntarily fill his eyes.

"Well, we don't know exactly," said the uniformed man.

"Men came here today, marched straight up these stairs, and then kicked in the door to your room," said Mr. Wrench. "We rehung it, but it doesn't shut right. It shuts of course but not right."

"Men?" Joel was confused.

"An Indian fellow and two others," said a man in the foyer. "I saw them myself. The Indian should be easy to identify, with all the tattoos on his face."

Joel now recovered what the men in the carriage had said.

"What happened to my father?" Joel asked, gravity now drawing his tears down his cheeks. He didn't want to say it, but it just tumbled out, "Is he dead?"

"No, no, we do not think that he is dead," said the uniformed man. "What we *know* is that he was here and now he is not."

"What am I to do?" Joel asked. "We must find my father."

"Once the Magistrate and Sheriff have cleared the room, and the undertaker is finished, I will have staff clean up and you can stay in your room tonight," said Mr. Wrench.

"Undertaker?" Joel said, "I thought that you said that my father was not dead."

"*He* is not dead, son, but..."

"Tom is dead!" said Mr. Wrench. "He was in the room when the men assaulted the door."

"Tom's corpse is up there just to be clear," said a man in the foyer.

BEAUTIFUL TOM WAS DEAD!

# 29

The Magistrate and Sherriff descended the stairs. They reached the floor. The Sherriff looked at Mr. Wrench and said, "Is this the boy?"

"Yes," said Mr. Wrench.

The Sherriff placed his hand on Joel's shoulder, "Son, I am sorry about all this. I would like to ask you a few questions." He looked at Mr. Wrench and asked, "Is there a place around here where the boy and I can talk?"

"Please," said Mr. Wrench motioning to his left, "the dining room is yours."

"Thank you," said the Sherriff. "After the undertaker removes the body from the premises, you can use the room again. Probably best to keep guests outside a while longer." He guided Joel by the shoulder into the dining room and motioned for him to sit. Mr. Wrench closed the French doors, separating the room off from the busy foyer.

The Sherriff pulled out a small book filled with notes and found an empty page. He pulled a pencil from an inside pocket of his coat. "What's your name, son?"

"Joel Hart, Sir," Joel said.

"Who is the man with whom you are staying upstairs?"

"My father. His name is Ephraim Hart. We're from New York City," Joel answered.

"Do you have a mother?"

"Yes, Sir. Francis Hart. My father is actually my stepfather."

"Is your mother here?"

"No, Sir. She is in Germany. She is taking care of her sick father."

"Is there anyone back home I can contact who can serve as a temporary guardian?"

"My Uncle Yusuf."

The Sherriff continued scribbling.

"Yusuf, you say?"

"Yes, Sir."

"Know how to spell that?"

"Like it sounds, I think."

The Sherriff smiled.

"Just Yusuf?"

"No, Sir. Yusuf is his last name. I think that his full name is Sheikh Yusuf."

"Okay, I won't ask how to spell that. Do you have an address for you uncle?"

"No, Sir. But he does spend a lot of time at the Tontine Coffee House with Misses Tontine. She does his laundry, and he wears her robe."

The Sherriff smiled again.

"What brought you and your father to Albany?"

"Business, Sir," Joel said.

"What sort of business?"

"My father and I came up here to see what was going on with the canal project. We—well, my father and uncle—sold stock in the canal company to many investors in New York City and word came the next day through Mister Simmons that the Western Inland Navigation Lock Company had filed papers that it was about to go out of business," Joel said. Thus far everything he had said was true. Even so, he was aware that he hadn't told the Sherriff *everything*. He then asked, "Is Tom really dead?" The tears came again.

"How did you know Tom?"

"I met him at the warehouse out on the dock when we arrived," answered Joel.

"How long ago was that?"

"Two days ago. On Thursday."

"Had you seen Tom since the time you met at the dock?"

"Yes, Sir," Joel said. "We met at the warehouse Friday morning, and we had lunch—sausages."

"And that was the last time you saw him?"

"No, Sir. He took me this morning on the barge up to the canal site. That was where I was coming from tonight."

"So, Tom was with you at the canal site?"

"Yes, Sir. But not all day. After he showed me around he had to leave to go to work at the materials depot there."

"So, he works at the warehouse and at the materials depot at the canal site?"

"That's what he told me, but..." Joel paused.

"But what, son?"

"When I couldn't board the barge to return to Albany, before I was going to walk back on the road along the river, I went to the materials depot to find Tom, but no one had ever heard of him."

"You believe that Tom did not work there?"

"That's what they said, yes, Sir."

"Why do you think he told you that he worked there?"

"Dunno, Sir."

"Why do you think he was up in your room this evening?"

"Dunno, Sir."

"So, after learning that Tom did not work there, you walked here from the camp?"

"No, Sir. A coachman let me ride on the running board of his carriage."

"Know his name?"

"No, Sir."

"Would you know why anyone would want to harm you or your father?"

"No, Sir," Joel said.

"Know why anyone would want to harm Tom?"

"No, Sir."

The Sherriff saw something in Joel's demeaner that suggested otherwise. "I get the sense, son, that you might have a theory."

"Yes, Sir, but it doesn't involve Tom," Joel admitted with some reluctance.

"I'd greatly appreciate your sharing it."

"Well, while I was riding on the running board, on the carriage on my way back tonight, I mean, I overheard men in the carriage say that folks were aware of our coming here to Albany to investigate the canal project, and that they were set on deterring that. They specifically said that Mister Morris and his Indian were among those determined to do that."

"Mister Morris and his Indian?"

"Yes, Sir. Mister Gouverneur Morris and his hencher, an Algonquin warrior mercenary."

The Sherriff scribbled. His eyebrows raised.

"Goooveneeer?" the Sherriff sounded out slowly. "Do you know how to spell that? Odd name."

"No, Sir. It *is* odd."

The Sherriff smiled and grunted a laugh. "And his Indian hencher, you say?"

"He has tattoos on his face."

"And why do you think Mister Morris and his Indian would want to harm you and your father? Does not sound like you or your father were in any real position to do anything to interfere with the canal project."

"I think that they don't want to bring any attention to what they're *really* doing."

"And what might that be?"

"The men in the carriage said that Mister Morris is here to recover gold bullion that the British Army hid up there somewhere near the Mohawk, during the war. The canal project is supposed to be a ruse. It's cover to what they're really doing."

The Sherriff stopped writing and looked Joel directly in the eyes. "The men in the carriage said this?"

"Yes, Sir."

"Do you know who these men were?"

"No, Sir."

"Could you describe them?"

"No, Sir. I never got a look. They were already in the carriage when I jumped on."

"What did the carriage look like?"

Joel tried to recollect it, but it was dark, and he never thought that it was something that he'd ever need to remember.

"It was black, a gentleman's carriage, I think, and it was pulled by two horses, one black the other white. I do recall that it had red spoked wheels. Oh, and it had a placard on the door that said *Excelsior*."

There was a knock at the door. Mr. Wrench entered the room.

"The Undertaker and Magistrate say the room is clear," Mr. Wrench reported. "I have instructed staff to clean up a bit and to put it back in order. The door is still akilter, but it shuts."

"Thank you, Mister Wrench," said the Sherriff.

"Can I get either of you something to eat or drink?"

"Nothing for me," answered the Sherriff. He looked at Joel. "Son, you must be hungry."

Joel realized that he was.

"Yes, Sir," he replied. He turned to Mr. Wrench, "Thank you, Mister Wrench, I would be grateful."

"I will have our cook make a plate for you."

As Mr. Wrench was closing the French doors, the Sherriff said, "Before you go, Mister Wrench, if it isn't too much of an imposition, I would very much like to interview you before I leave tonight."

"Me?" said Mr. Wrench in an unexpected falsetto.

"Yes, if it's no trouble," said the Sherriff.

"No, of course not. No trouble at all."

The Sherriff looked at Joel. "I think that we can stop for now. I want to impress upon you that you must share with no one anything you shared with me."

"Yes, Sir."

"No one." The Sherriff's eyes ever so slighted shifted in the direction of Mr. Wrench.

"Yes, Sir."

"Would you like me to take you up to your room?"

"No, Sir. Thank you."

"One of my Deputies will be right outside your door. No one will harm you. If you need anything, you can tell the Deputy."

"What about my father?"

"I have men looking for him now."

"And Tom?"

The Sherriff looked away.

Joel felt shame in feeling relief that it was Tom and not him who had been killed.

"If that is all," said Mr. Wrench, "I'll get things started with the cook." He quickly shut the doors.

The Sherriff looked at Joel again. "Do you trust that one?"

"Mister Wrench?"

"Yes, Mister Wrench."

"He has been nice so far, but..."

"But what?"

"Tom had told me not to trust what he had to say about him."

"Did you get the sense that Tom and Mister Wrench did not like one another?"

"Yes, Sir."

"I will leave you now, young Joel, but I want to follow up with you on what you heard when riding on your carriage. Try to recall more if you can."

"Yes, Sir."

"If we find your father, I'll send someone here to tell you. For now, I will send word to your uncle."

"Thank you."

The Sherriff pocketed his pencil and little book, pounded his palms rather forcefully onto the table, got up and exited the room. Joel could still see through the open doors several people lingering in the foyer. He leaned back and saw out a window that most of the crowd out on the street had dispersed.

# 30

Although Mr. Wrench's staff had put the room back together, Joel, the moment he entered the room, was hit with a strong musky odor—not the oder of a human being, but the smell of a cornered animal. The room was saturated with it.

Tom was dead.

How was this possible? He had just seen him this morning, just spoke to him, had just encountered him there in his face, his eyes, in the way he moved and walked.

Tom was dead.

Joel thought it odd that he could still feel Tom's presence. Was this his spirit lingering on earth, in this room? Joel was frightened to let the room go dark, so he made sure to put the extra candles kept in the dresser drawer on the nightstand in case he needed to replace the ones currently burning in their holders. He could still see Tom in his imagination, alive. But

Tom was dead.

The thought was so strange. For, at one moment it would feel simply as though Tom had left, perhaps had gone off to sea, where he and Joel would be separated by miles of black ocean. Joel might not see Tom ever again. But in such a scenario, they at least *could* see one another, for both were still inhabitants of the earth. That thought was now being assaulted by the realization that this was *not* the state of things. Tom was not at sea. Tom was no longer alive. He was no longer on this earth. He was on a ship that could *never* return to any port. The very possibility of Joel's never seeing Tom again threatened to unravel Joel's sense of reality itself.

Joel cried an unexpected deep cry at the thought of Tom lying here in this room, of Tom's being no more. The last thing he saw was this room. The last thing he would ever see was this room. Surely Tom had plans for a future, for a family. But there would never be a future for

Tom. How final. How terrifyingly final and yet ridiculously mundane that he died here in a room at the Iron Horse. The thought was charged with magnetic opposites. Why was he here in this room? What had happened? Did you struggle, Tom? Did you suffer pain? Did you think in your final moments of your family? Your mother? Me?

Tom was dead.

The thought now ruled over Joel's mind. He could not escape it. As soon as he would recollect the beautiful Tom, the possibility of love, Pausanias' speech, in trying to inject something positive into the world, the dreadful thought would break in.

Tom was dead.

Joel imagined him lying on the floor. Dead. Eyes open. Very likely his final breath still lingered in the room. Joel was frightened to breath it in, afraid that that would complete Tom's journey, and Tom would be gone forever. But he *was* gone forever.

Tom was dead.

What happens to someone when they die? Do we continue? Or are we annihilated completely? Joel felt like a character in Plato's *Phaedo*. He wished Plato was here to help him answer these questions. The dialogue was no longer a piece of juvenal entertainment but would now serve as a great map of life.

But then more urgent questions sounded through his grief. Where was his father? Where was Hart? Joel could not imagine Hart lying dead somewhere. It was more than his sixteen-year-old soul could bear. Did the hencher take his father? For what purpose? Did Hart escape the henchman's deadly grasp? Clearly, poor Tom did not. Or, had Tom been with the Indian and it was Hart who killed Tom and then fled the Iron Horse? The thought was a flat-out contradiction though it tried to form in Joel's noggin. Hart could *never* kill a man. And, if he was forced to, perhaps out of self-defense, he would have surely remained so as to properly report it to the authorities. No, Hart had to be the prey here, not the predator. But if Hart had escaped the hencher, why had he not returned to the Iron Horse when the Sherriff and Magistrate arrived? Surely he had to know that the assault, the kicking in of the door, would have stirred the summoning of authorities. He would have been safe. If he had escaped, where was he now?

The clock in the hall sounded three bells, marking three in the morning. The evening had passed so quickly. Joel could not sleep. He would not sleep. He could hear the floor creak outside his door whenever the Deputy shifted his weight. He lay on the bed and stared at the shadows that danced on the walls and ceiling. He could see faces, he could even see the tragedy played out in the room, and yet he knew that he was really seeing none of this. He thought of the stillness in the eyes of the man on the barge. He saw strength in that stillness. As he imagined how this man acquired that stillness, Joel felt the hypnotic rhythm of the barge as it moved upriver, and eventually a temporary calm in the storm found him there the bed, and he fell into a deep sleep.

# 31

Joel awoke to the sound of the door creaking open. It was the Deputy.

"Good morning, young man," said the Deputy.

For a moment everything felt normal, but then Joel was assaulted by the thought of the violence that had transpired last night.

A bit of a commotion was occurring downstairs. The Deputy turned to see what was happening. Joel could hear a man and someone who sounded like Mr. Wrench arguing. He heard the one man say, "Señor, necesito hablar con Chole Hart." It was Ignacio! Joel immediately jumped from the bed and went to the door, but the Deputy stood his ground and would not let Joel pass. He heard Mr. Wrench say, "Young man speak English. Do you know English? You are in American now; we only speak *English*!" Another man spoke out, a Dutch local, "Ik spreek naast Engels ook Nederlands, en ik ben een Amerikaan. Het grootste deel van de dag spreek ik Nederlands, you idiot!" Several men in the sitting room laughed. Joel only understood the "you idiot" bit. But the man's point seemed to be that men speak many languages in America.

Joel called down to Ignacio, "Iggy, write a note and Mister Wrench can give it to the Deputy up here and he will pass it along to me."

"I will allow it," said the Deputy loud enough for Mr. Wrench to hear.

"You hab pen on peper?" Iggy asked Mr. Wrench.

"Pen and paper? Yes, I can get those for you," said Mr. Wrench.

"I gib note. Come me see leter, Chole," said Ignacio.

Mr. Wrench ascended the stairs. Joel saw that he was reading the note. He folded it back in the manner in which Ignacio had given it and handed it to the Deputy. He handed the folded note to Joel, and said to Mr. Wrench, "Did the young man leave?"

"Yes, thank the gods," answered Mr. Wrench.

The Deputy turned to Joel and told him to get dressed and that he would get Mr. Wrench to have breakfast brought up to the room.

Joel closed the door and opened the note. It read:

> the man hoo u no namd afdr es a mi casa—creo que nuestro amigo Tom está muerto

Ignacio was saying that Hart was hiding aboard Ignacio's ship!

Should he tell the Deputy? The Sherriff? Or should he wait, go to the ship, and find out from Hart what had happened? It was difficult to know who could be trusted. Luckily, Ignacio had put enough of the message in broken English and Spanish that may have prevented Mr. Wrench from deciphering it.

# 32

The Deputy reported that the Sherriff's men had still not found Joel's father but were still looking. Word was that the hencher and his men had fled deep into the Catskills and would likely not be of any threat to Joel, at least not for the next couple of days. The Deputy said that he was going to go home, and another would arrive on duty sometime around supper. In the interim, Joel was supposed to stay at the Iron Horse. If he did venture out, he was on his own. Mr. Wrench had instructions on what to do were the hencher and his men to return.

After the Deputy departed, Joel planned to sneak out of the Iron Horse and make his way to Ignacio's ship. But Mr. Wrench kept a rather close watch of Joel's whereabouts. Joel knew that there was a large window in the reading room. Perhaps he could sneak out through it when Mr. Wrench's duties were most demanding. By the time Mr. Wrench got around to locating him, Joel should have returned to the Iron Horse.

As Joel made his way down the stairs, where he planned to let Mr. Wrench know that he would be in the reading room, he saw Ignacio silhouetted in the foyer. He was accompanied by the silhouette of a woman.

"Ignacio?" Joel said.

"Jes, et es Ignacio, Meester Chole Hart," Ignacio said rather formally, appearing to perform for those guests in the sitting room off to his right and dining room off to his left, "an et es mi pleasure for you to met mi Tía." He turned and bowed and gestured with his arms as though introducing the Queen.

Mr. Wrench entered from one of the hallways that run along the sides of the staircase. "Young man, I thought I had told you not to return here."

"It is okay, Mister Wrench, this is my friend Ignacio," Joel said. "And this is his...?"

"Tía," said Ignacio. He repeated his introducing the Queen act.

"Where is the Deputy when you need him?" Mr. Wrench said.

"Please, Mister Wrench, I assure you that Ignacio meant no disrespect last night. He was just concerned for me, that's all."

"Es verdad, I waz aconcerned for heem, Señor," Ignacio confirmed.

"Well the lot of you can visit on the porch, then," said Mr. Wrench. "Remember, Master Joel, the Sherriff says that you must stay at the Iron Horse. The porch is as far as you go."

"Yes, Sir. Thank you, Mister Wrench," Joel said.

The three of them went out the tall front doors and found a place to linger at the far end of the porch.

"This is not your...what did call her?" Joel said in a whisper.

"Mi Tía," Ignacio answered. "She es as you say mi ontie."

"This is not your aunt," Joel said. "You are from Spain. You told me that you have no family in America."

"You imbecile, it's me, your father!" said the woman with a deep voice.

Joel could not believe his eyes. He examined the heavily powdered face. It *was* Hart!

"Where did you get those clothes?" Joel asked. "The wig is..."

"Day es mine, amigo," said Ignacio.

"Yours?"

"When ships cross the equator," Lady Hart said, "it's apparently a tradition to haze the young men and especially those who have never crossed before, as a kind of initiation, by making them dress like women, dance, and entertain the crew. Tawdry stuff to hear him and his crew tell of it."

"Deez es mi vestido I bot," Ignacio said, "I no hab to dress up no longer, seense I, cómo se dice, he cruzado el Ecuador, pero I steel hab vestidos for the new boyz. I a sharges dem to wear estos vesitdos. Es a barry good, cómo se dice, negocio."

"We figured that it was safer if I wore this disguise," Hart explained.

"Tom is dead," Joel said, grief returned to his face.

"I know," said Hart, stung by seeing Joel hurt so deeply. "He saved my life."

"Tom?"

"He showed up to our room and warned me that several men were on their way to kill us. He said that he had known about the plot since Friday night. He took you to the canal site to get you clear of the city and returned to warn me. The men came into the Iron Horse, and they saw me with Tom, and we moved into the room and locked the door, but they ran up to the room and kicked in the door. Tom told me to go out the window. I was about halfway out, and Tom stood between me and the men. The last I saw..." Hart's bloodshot eyes filled with tears.

"The last you saw?" Joel pleaded.

"The last I saw was the hencher taking Tom by the throat. I felt sick. I fell ass-first out the window onto the tin roof of the building next door and then fell off that into the back alley. I'm pretty banged up underneath this exquisite apparel. I ran to the town square thinking that perhaps I would be safer in a public setting. That's when Ignacio here saw me. He had been instructed by Tom to await our arrival. I told him what had just happened, and without any concern for his own safety, he bravely took me to his ship."

"It waz no so brave, mi Tía," said Ignacio, looking at Joel and making a sign of the cross.

"No, Iggy, you are a *hero*!" said Joel. He embraced Ignacio and then reached out and pulled the Lady Hart by her fake boob into the hug. The three of them sobbed for some time about Tom.

Joel caught a glimpse of Mr. Wrench spying on the three of them through one of the large dining room windows. He slipped out of sight when he detected Joel's glimpse.

"How did Tom discover the plot, I wonder?" asked Joel as he wiped his cheeks.

"Your Uncle Yusuf sent a message to us, which was the post brought along with us on our ship—remember, the letter that Tom delivered? That letter warned of Mister Morris' presence. He must have written it after we boarded. Why the captain didn't just give it to us on the ship is a mystery."

"So, you never wrote a letter to the Iron Horse to let them know of our arrival?" Joel asked.

"No, I did not send any letter. That was the letter from Yusuf. But when Mister Wrench pulled the letter out of his bag, I was more than a little surprised. I thought for a second there that I was like a wizard or something. When Mister Wrench read it and acted like it *was* the letter I had sent, I knew that something was afoot, my possible magical abilities aside, but I did not know what to make of it. I thought that maybe we got lucky and that someone else named Ephraim Hart had written a letter announcing his arrival. Pretty low odds that, but, hey, I've seen weirder. Anyway, you will recall that Mister Wrench kept the letter. He didn't give it to me. It was addressed to me, not to him. Of course, I didn't know that at the time, but Tom did. So, I did not know that Mister Morris was here until my visit to the canal site on Friday and Mister King told me all about our Mister Morris and his hencher. I believe that Morris must have seen me but feigned not to...to not see me, I mean."

"How did you find out that Uncle Yusuf had written the warning to us?" Joel asked. "Did Mister Wrench eventually give you the letter?"

"No. Tom delivered mail as usual on Friday, before supper, when I was returning from the canal visit and he saw you in the reading room. Mister Wrench was out, and Tom noticed that the letter he had delivered to us, the one that Mister Wrench took out of his bag, read, but kept for himself, was there serving as a bookmark in one of Mister Wrench's inventory books, in the kitchen, I think. Anyway, Tom read the letter and put it back. That evening, near the warehouse, he overheard several men discussing what was clearly a plot to kill you and me. Not to scare us or to run us out of town. To *kill* us! Their plan was to do the deed here in the Iron Horse, in broad daylight, which would terrify folks so much that none would visit Albany for a while."

"Tom said that he worked at the canal site. I found out that he didn't. He lied," Joel said.

"Yes, he told me, just before, you know, that he had told you that to impress you. From what I could gather, he thought that perhaps you'd take him up on his invitation to show you around the canal site. He surely would have told you the truth after we were out of harm's way. He didn't know that Mister Morris and his hencher had set up shop there at the canal site. He really didn't know much about them, but only that they were not really part of the canal project. He said that as he was leaving you to return to find me, the hencher and three men saw him and followed him back to the city. I don't think that he meant to lie to you, Joel. I think that he genuinely liked you and wanted you to like him."

"Es verdad, Chole Hart. Thomás waz a barry good mon. Creo que le gustaste," Ignacio said.

"Tom told me that your uncle's letter said that we must be careful, that men at the Tontine Coffee House had alerted people here, people who had ulterior motives for the canal, and that we were coming to muck the whole thing up. At all costs, our inquiry was to be buried here. I think that these men thought we were here to *save* the company. Ironic, you know, since that was not what we came here to do. They *want* to company to fail. I think that we should get out of here and let them finish the job. We'll be in the clear with those who we sold stocks to. And, if the thing does go under, we'll still be able to bring to fruition your plan. Your Uncle Yusuf will be happy to hear none of our dealings had any actual causal impact on the fall of the company. Unbeknownst to you and me, the company's failure was in the cards from the get-go, long before we borrowed and sold the stock."

The three adjusted their stances to draw less attention to themselves. Hart was careful not to wipe his makeup off. He adjusted his magnificent wig.

"When I was at the canal site, I saw Mister Morris and the hencher at the privies," Joel reported.

"Really?" Hart replied, "he must really like privies."

"No, that's not it," Joel leaned in. "I saw fifteen men emerge from a single outhouse."

"Feeteen? Thots a lot of mens, amigo," said Ignacio.

"I've seen clowns at circuses do similar things. Fifty-seven clowns in a carriage, I saw," said Hart.

"This was not a trick. I think that that outhouse is an entryway to an underground structure of some kind. It's an entryway disguised as an outhouse."

"Why on earth would anyone want an underground structure in a place of outhouses? Must reek," Hart said.

"Well then their ruse is working. Who *would* suspect an underground bunker there? But this fits into another piece of information that I overheard, which I am now realizing I forgot to mention," said Joel.

"What did you overhear?"

"When I decided to return from the canal site, I had to take the road back. The barge was full. That's when I went to find Tom at the materials depot, only to discover that no one there knew of him. That stunned me a bit. I was able to ride back to Albany on the running board of a small carriage. Three men in the carriage were talking about Mister Morris. That's when I heard rumor that's going around that there were two from New York City who had come to Albany to investigate the lock company, that Mister Morris was on to that information and was aiming to interfere with the investigation. They knew that the two were a man and his daughter—well, son...a daughter dressed as a son—whatever—and that Mister Morris had plans to eliminate them. Something to that effect."

"Sounds ominous. I'd hate to be those two," Hart said.

Joel and Ignacio gave a stern look.

"I'm just trying to lighten this up. I know that in this story we are the man and his daughter."

"Ahora una Tía y su sobrino," Ignacio said.

"Good one," Hart said.

Joel stood aghast at Hart's newly acquired ability to understand Spanish. He shook his head. "My plan was that once at the Iron Horse, I'd find you and tell you what I had heard. But as I approached the inn, I saw everyone out on the porch and in the street, and it is all a blur from there."

"So, Morris wanted to stop us from *investigating* the company. Clearly, he doesn't know that we were here to do something much worse really, so that's good," Hart said. "But killing a father and his daughter for just looking into the workings of a lock company, which is all he thought we were doing, doesn't seem like the sort of thing that calls for *murder*."

"I think I forgot to mention the gold bullion," Joel said.

# 33

"Gold bullion!" Lady Hart said a bit too loudly, in a baritone voice no less. Several guests talking on the other side of the porch stopped what they were doing and gawked.

"Lo siento," said Ignacio trying to match the deep voice.

The gawkers acknowledged the apology and returned to their conversation.

"Perhaps I should have put the bullion thing at the beginning of my story," Joel admitted.

"You think?" said Lady Hart.

The three stared at one another for a moment.

"Chole an Ontie Hart," Ignacio interjected, "et es known dat d'Englich heed monies all d'over d'coast. I hab a seen dees befor. Al norte de aqui."

"I have read about that, too," Hart said.

"You followed all of that?" asked Joel.

"Of course," Hart answered. "Pirates are also known for hiding treasure in this manner."

"Jes, d'pirates," Ignacio confirmed. "I hab aheard dat d'Knights Templars do dis también," he said while making the sign of the cross.

"The men in the carriage said that the canal project is simply cover for recovering the bullion," Joel said. "Once the gold is recovered, the lock company's demise is not far behind. Maybe we should just get out of here, like you said, and let the powers that be do our work for us."

"Yes, and it doesn't look much like cover at this point anyway," said Hart. "I get the sense that the big hole up at Cohoes is solely the result of those men having been looking for the gold all along. But you're right, there is really nothing that we need to do here. The deed we set out to do was in the doing before we arrived."

"Pero necesitamos vengar a Tom!" Ignacio insisted.

"Yes," said Hart, "we must avenge Tom!"

"Seriously—you understood that?" Joel asked.

"Before we head back home," Lady Hart said, "we must secure justice for Tom. I for one will not be able to live with myself if we do not at least try!"

# 34

"Dey es a Lady we must beeseet befor we proceed to de avenging," said Ignacio. "She will gib us aguidance."

"We will have to divert Mister Wrench's attention if I am to escape the Iron Horse," Joel noted.

"Ontie Hart and mi hab dat cobered, mi amigo," Ignacio said. He produced from his satchel a large bag. "Take dees to da room up astair and shanges into dees."

Joel took the bag and peeked inside.

"No, you cannot be serious," Joel said.

"We couldn't be more serious," Lady Hart assured.

Hart swatted Joel firmly on the bum and said in the best falsetto he could muster, "Now, go, little one. Your Auntie Hart commands it."

Joel went back inside, up the wide staircase, and into his room with the creaky door.

Mr. Wrench appeared on the porch.

"Would either of you like something?" Wrench asked.

"No, Señor, gracias," Ignacio replied.

"The lady?"

"No, thank you," Hart replied in falsetto as she produced a fan and placed it between her face and Mr. Wrench's gaze.

"Well, on your way then," Wrench said, gesturing to the street.

"Jes, Señor Hwrench, we hweel be on our hway," answered Ignacio.

Mr. Wrench stood patiently in a half bow pose, awaiting their exit from the porch.

"We should go, nephew," said Lady Hart to Ignacio. She took Ignacio's hand and together they strolled off the porch and into the street. Mr. Wrench asked the gawkers who were still lingering on the porch whether they needed anything, they shook their heads to indicate "no," and he disappeared back into the Iron Horse. Ignacio and Lady Hart found a place directly behind an enormous coach that would hide them from Mr. Wrench's view were he to gander out one of the front windows of the Iron Horse. Ignacio kept a lookout for the soon-to-be-disguised Joel through the spokes of one of the coach's rear wheels.

After a good twenty minutes, Joel appeared. She was even more beautiful than Ignacio's Tía. She stood on the porch looking for her companions. Ignacio gave a ridiculously loud whistle. So loud, in fact, the coach's team of horses lurched forward, waking the coachman from his nap, who instinctively calmed them down with a "Whoa," and the gawkers began gawking again. Joel looked in the direction of the whistle and Ignacio and Lady Hart appeared from behind the monstrous coach.

"Ju looked abeautiful," said Ignacio with a smile.

"Shut up," answered Joel, "but having seen myself in the mirror I must admit that I do."

"So, Ignacio, where is this lady you insist on seeing, and why is it that we must see her exactly?" asked Lady Hart.

"Eber seense I ahab a ben beeseetin here, befor I do someteen adangerous, I beeseet dis a lady," Ignacio answered. "She es, cómo se dice, una bruha."

"A witch?" Lady Hart gasped.

"Maybees ju call her instead a psychic?" Ignacio clarified.

"A psychic?" Joel gasped. "Like a fortuneteller or something?"

"Jes, dat sounds aright!"

"Why must we see your fortuneteller?" Lady Hart asked.

"She weel ahelp us abenging Tom."

Ignacio led the two ladies into the more seedy part of Albany, near the docks, where dockworkers, sailors, and prostitutes commune. As they worked down Front Street, whistles could be heard coming from the moored ships, as tokens of appreciation for the two beauties who accompanied Ignacio.

The three arrived at a large house. The sign on the porch read FIGHTIN' COCKS.

"We've got one of these back home. Americans sure like their cock fightings," said Lady Hart.

"Good chicken," Joel added.

"Yes, good chicken."

Just as Lady Hart said this, two men tumbled in wild embrace out of the front doors onto the porch. Laughter from those inside grew. The two men appeared to be fighting, though they seemed too drunk for anything more than rolling around on the porch in a passionate embrace.

"Fightin' cocks," Ignacio said with a laugh.

"Your fortuneteller is in there?" asked Joel.

"Jes, en dere, Chole Hart."

They walked up the steps to the porch, at which time the two huggers parted, stood up though a bit wobblily, brushed themselves off, and said, "Ladies," tilting imaginary hats. Both had wide smiles, though few teeth.

The three entered the Fightin' Cocks. It was very dark inside, lit by few whale oil lanterns. A stark contrast to the open, breezy, and well-lit Iron Horse. Many chatty bodies occupied every ground floor room they could see—some drinking, some gambling—no one paid any attention to Lady Hart or Joel. Several men sitting somewhere in the back yelled out "Ignacio!" and he raised his arm and smile in the direction of the calls.

They snaked their way through the dense gathering and found a hallway in the back that led to another, which required a short climb of stairs, and from the looks of it they had entered another building, which was even darker and noticeably colder. Ignacio led them to a room whose doorway was a curtain of metallic beads. Joel noticed that he felt something odd as he approached it. The hair on his arms stood up.

Ignacio gestured for the two to enter. Lady Hart approached the metallic curtain and it parted without her touching it. Strange. Joel's "feeling" grew stronger as though prompted by the movement of the curtain.

The room smelled lightly of sulfur. Though within a second or two the odor was no longer detected. Standing at the far end of the room was a woman who must have stood seven feet tall. Was this a dream?

The woman wore a tall wig, which accentuated her height, but was remarkably slender with very long arms. She wore a veil; even so, Lady Hart could see her eyes, which appeared to be large and black. Each heard "sit" even though none saw her mouth move. This *was* a witch, Joel said to himself. But the thought dissolved, and he immediately felt at ease, the feeling very much like that felt from drinking the watered-down ale at the Iron Horse.

The three travelers sat at a large table that stood between them and the woman. She did not sit. Ignacio, who now appeared to be entranced, took from the table a deck of cards. They had drawings of all sorts of things on them, though recognizable were cups, batons, coins, and long swords—hearts, clubs, diamonds, and spades? Strange deck indeed.

Ignacio shuffled the cards three times and then divided them into four stacks. Using his left hand, he took the top card from each and placed each face down on the table. One card was at the top, and three below, making a single row. Ignacio turned the top card over, again with his left hand, which said LERMITE, this card numbered VIIII. Each "heard" the woman tell them that this card would provide context for the reading. In this case, it was THE HERMIT, a card that represents selfhood. It is number nine among the Major Arcana, the latter representing stages of one's life. THE HERMIT card represents a masculine energy and speaks of a temporary shut off from external influences while thought is given to one's identity. That self-discovery had been in play for some time now.

Their attention was drawn to the three cards just below THE HERMIT. The positions of the three cards represent the PAST, PRESENT, and FUTURE, respectively.

Ignacio turned over the first card in the row of three, on the left—the PAST. It was LA PANCES, number II in the Major Arcana. This card, THE PAPESSE, the female Pope, represents a feminine energy and speaks of one's studies and of the knowledge one acquires. It speaks of a trust in nature, science, and astronomy as guiding sources. Since this card appears in the PAST position, it indicates that what one has learned in the past and the continued pursuit of knowledge is important to understanding the significance of the card in the PRESENT position.

The PRESENT. Ignacio turned over the middle card. It was the CAVALIER de DENIERS. Ignacio said, "Caballero de Oro," at which time Lady Hart and Joel "heard," THE KNIGHT OF COINS. Joel was particularly drawn to the monetary aspect of this card's suit. The tall black-eyed woman expressed to Joel a warm smile.

The two were told that in the present they were engaged in a pursuit of *material* things, the suit of PENTACLES representing all aspects of materiality. The gold they now sought was not what they thought. The scheme to short the Western Inland Navigation Lock Company was a ruse their guides had employed to bring them here. The scheme had been planted in them when traveling through Penn's Woods. But the new scheme to thwart those seeking gold bullion was another ruse still. Ruses within ruses. Their being here had nothing to do with these things. The gold they would *find* would not be gold they could spend. The gold was nothing material but was something more precious, it was something they would *know*. It was brought to their attention that the Knight was heading in the direction of the third card, away from the past and toward the FUTURE.

The third card was turned face up. It was LE TOILE, number XVII of the Major Arcana. THE STAR. This represents a feminine energy.

A naked woman is pictured in a rather difficult kneeling position, one foot on earth the other in water. She is pouring water from two vessels, one onto the land and the other back into the small pool of water in which she stands. The card comes directly after THE TOWER card, the latter representing destruction, suggesting that she is not kneeling but *rising*. She represents what follows in the wake of such destruction—hope, insight, and a sense that one is being safely guided by benevolent forces in the universe.

Joel was immediately struck that the Knight of Gold, as Ignacio had put it, was the *hencher*. Yet, he wasn't a hencher. He held in his hand a staff. The staff turned into a long slender ivory needle. It was a bone from a whale. The hencher who was not a hencher extended his hand and gave it to Joel. He took it. Joel "heard" the woman say, "Whatever the one-legged man takes from you will take from him his own life." The hencher withdrew his hand and the card returned to the original depiction. But now the Knight looked like Tom.

Lady Hart and Joel found themselves standing with Ignacio back out on the street, in front of the Fightin' Cocks. Two men tumbled out of the front doors onto the porch. Hadn't they seen this before? What was going on? None among the three could recall how they got outside. They were in the inner sanctum one moment with the strange woman and standing here the next. The repeat of the two huggers tumbling onto the porch only added to the confusion of what had happened. Had what they thought had happened, happened?

Lady Hart said, "We must go to the privies at Cohoes."

"You're telling me," Joel said. "I may have already done the deed in my dress."

"No, I mean, there is something in that outhouse you spied that we *must* see."

"Yes, I feel as though that is where the gold is," Joel agreed.

"Yes, the gold," said Lady Hart.

"Pero el oro que no es oro," Ignacio reminded the two.

# 35

The three made their way to the road that runs parallel to the Hudson. It was safer, they thought, to travel north by carriage than by crowded barge.

Lady Hart secured a small gentleman's carriage and the three climbed aboard.

The road during the day was very busy, something that Joel had not himself witnessed since the only time he had ventured upriver during daytime was on the barge. To those on the river, the road lay hidden behind several rows of large trees. The cicadas continued composing their epic song of longing.

"I am still a bit unsettled about what we just experienced," said Lady Hart.

"The fortuneteller?" asked Joel.

"Of course, you dimwit."

"You'd think that the both of us dressed like ladies would be on the top of that list," Joel said. "But I must admit, the fortuneteller tops even that."

"Dot waz abit ascary, I mus admit, Ontie Hart," Ignacio said.

"You seemed to know what you were doing with those cards," Joel said.

"Doing?" asked Ignacio.

"You know, when you took the cards from the table, shuffled them, laid them out, and then turned them over for the fortuneteller to read?" Joel said.

"I deed dat? I tot dat *you* did a dat?"

"I thought that *I* did that," said Lady Hart.

"That *is* strange," said Joel.

"Dat *eez* so astrange," Ignacio agreed.

"How do you even know that lady?" Joel asked.

"Eber seense I been beeseetin here, fibe years maybe, I know her," Ignacio said.

"Five years?" Lady Hart asked.

"Jes, I come here once a year. El barco es de mi Tío. La mujer tiene mil años!"

"She's a thousand years old? I don't know why, but it makes sense," said Lady Hart. "Why take *us* to see her?"

"Mi Tío tiene a relation con los angeles del mar. Dey sabed heez life, cómo se dice, hwen d'boat es at sea. Wheneber we moor aquí, he es obligated to pay heez respects to her—Elle es un ángel del mar! Elle come to mi en un sueño anoche. She tolded mi to bring you to her."

"She didn't look...she didn't look *human*, no disrespect, but there, I said it. Though I must admit that the further we are getting from our time at the Fightin' Cocks the less I can recall details of her face. She was very tall, yes?" Lady Hart asked.

"Yes," said Joel, "taller than my giant."

"Tu gigante?" asked Ignacio.

"Mister Morris," Joel answered. "He was tall too."

"Nuestro pegleg Señor Morris?"

"No, a different massively headed Señor Morris. They are not related," said Joel.

"Oh, coz I waz a gonna say that Señor Morris waz not so beeg."

"On account of his pegleg," asked Lady Hart.

"No, Ontie Hart, coz ob heez size."

"There was something about her eyes, don't you think?" asked Lady Hart.

"Chilling," answered Joel. "Large and black."

"Si grande y Negra."

"Although I could hear her, I actually never saw her mouth move," added Joel.

"Chilling," said Lady Hart. "I had thought the same."

"Elle habla con su mente," Ignacio explained. "Ella habla muy bien español.

"Spanish? You mean English, no?"

"No, I mean español, Chole Hart."

"So she *is* a witch!" said Lady Hart. "To Ignacio she speaks Spanish, to us English."

"Una bruja o un ángel, lo mismo, I tink," Ignacio said.

"The gold we seek is not gold? Do I recall that right?" asked Lady Hart.

"Jes, Ontie Hart, ju recalls dot right."

"What does that mean, I wonder?"

"I got the sense," Joel speculated, "that we were being told that the gold we were seeking was *knowledge*. But I am not aware of any knowledge that I could possess that would be as good as gold. At least that is what came to mind when she told us that."

"Creo que el conocimiento se trata de quiénes y qué somos. Ese fue mi pensamiento," Ignacio said.

"Yes, that was my sense too," said Lady Hart, "The knowledge of who and what we *are*. Strange to even think it. Sounds so biblical."

"I'm still hoping that we're talking gold—the kind I can take to the bank!" added Joel. But as he said this, he realized that this was the old Joel speaking. As this adventure had unfolded, Joel felt that such knowledge would be worth *everything*, even more than gold bullion. It was the sort of knowledge that Socrates sought. Joel could not believe that he was thinking this thought.

The three sat silently for several minutes in a kind of stupor.

"I saw the knight change into the hencher. Though, what was weird was that he was the hencher and not the hencher at the same time," Joel said.

"Logically impossible, I'm afraid," said Lady Hart.

"And yet it made sense at the time. He was holding a staff of some sort but then it turned into a very long needle-like object. I think it was a whale bone?"

"Did the hencher poke you with it?" asked Lady Hart.

"He gave it to me, and then I heard the woman say that whatever Mister Morris takes from me will be that which takes his life."

"That's creepy," Lady Hart said. "I don't recall her saying that—at least not to me."

"Jes, dot es acreepy Chole Hart," Ignacio confirmed. "I no heard dat neither."

"Do you have the whale bone on you?" asked Lady Hart. "I mean, if you did, that would be physical evidence against thinking it was all a hallucination."

"I don't think so," Joel felt around his dress

"Es dat eet?" Ignacio said while reaching at something in Joel's tall wig.

He pulled out what appeared to be a long hairpin.

"That's it!" Joel exclaimed.

"Evidence!" Lady Hart said excitedly. "Are you supposed to stab the hencher who is not a hencher with it?"

"Dunno," said Joel, "But I don't think so."

They heard the driver call out to the horses and the carriage began slowing down. It stopped, and a moment later the driver was opening the door. "Ladies, gentleman, we have arrived at Cohoes."

# 36

The three followed the wide road to the canal site. Several men tipped hats to Lady Hart, almost always accompanied with a smile.

"Over there," said Joel, "do you see them?"

"See hwhat?" asked Ignacio.

"The privies. There."

"Ju mean dose little houzes?"

"Which one is the one?" asked Lady Hart.

"The only one with the man in front standing guard," Joel said.

"Are you sure that he's standing guard? He could just be waiting his turn."

"There are several unoccupied outhouses. Look! Their doors are wide open. If he needed to go..." Joel said.

"Yes, I see your point," Lady Hart replied. "What is your plan?"

"To get into that door," Joel said, "But we will first need to distract the guard."

Unbeknownst to the boys, the very disguises they were wearing were the very thing they could employ to pull off the distraction.

"Don't look," said Lady Hart, "but I think that our guard is ogling us."

Joel turned to see.

"I said don't look! What part of 'don't look' do you not understand?"

"I understond 'don look,' Ontie Hart. I am no looking," said Ignacio. He did his best to see the guard from the corner of his eyes.

"What are you doing?" asked Lady Hart.

"No looking at heem," Ignacio said.

"Give me your fan," said Joel. He snatched the fan from Lady Hart, opened it and peered over the top edge. The guard *was* ogling.

"You hab your deestraction, I tink."

"Yes, the man has an eye for the ladies," Lady Hart surmised.

"Or for men in ladies' clothes," Joel said.

"Even more interesting if I'm being honest," said Lady Hart. She paused and then said, "I don't know about you, but I am rather enjoying this apparel. I only wish that men could get away with wearing such things. Wigs, make up, stylish blouses, stockings, and shoes."

"Are you serious? It's the eighteenth century, sister. You just described almost every man we know back home," Joel said.

"Touché!" said Lady Hart.

"You have like what...three wigs?"

"A few more than that I think," said Lady Hart.

"I deed not know dat. You hab a *hweegs* Ontie Hart?" asked Ignacio.

"Several."

"You no hab wheeg when I see you dees days."

"I save them for special social occasions," Lady Hart said. "I don't wear them daily like some. And I did not bring any on this trip."

"Touché," Ignacio said.

"That's not a *touché* moment, my Ignacio," Lady Hart said.

"To use *touché* the person needs to have said something in reply to something you said that was *clever*, something that counters what you said," Joel explained. "Nothing that your auntie just said was clever."

"Touché," Ignacio said.

"Okay, we'll work on that later," said Lady Hart.

The three posed their best poses, trying to appear unaware of the ogling, though posing to produce more of it if such was possible.

"Let's say that we distract your guard," Lady Hart said, "what is your plan for what we will do once we are in the outhouse underground bunker? Do you have a plan for how we will remove the gold? Gold is heavy—*very* heavy."

"First, let me modify *distract*," Joel said. "The guard needs to be *out* of the picture, not simply distracted."

"You're not suggesting that we *kill* him!" Lady Hart said.

"No, no, you imbecile, just conked out for a bit," Joel replied.

"Conkeded out? I hab no heard dees before," said Ignacio.

"Knocked unconscious," said Lady Hart, miming a punch and being knocked out.

"Ju mean like make asleep?"

"Yes, we need to make him sleep."

The three thought about how to do that.

"I will visit the outhouse next to his and ask him to help me with my dress," said Joel.

"That sounds scandalous," Lady Hart replied.

"Exactly," said Joel. "Which means the guy deserves to be conked out if he's so willing to help a lady in that way. So, we should not feel so guilty. I will lure him just into the outhouse when one of you will conk him on the noggin. We'll leave him to sleep it off in the outhouse."

Joel looked around and found a palm-sized stone.

"Use this to do the conking," Joel said, handing the stone to Ignacio, who handed it to Lady Hart.

"I don't want to conk him," Lady Hart insisted.

"I no wan to either," said Ignacio. "I hate biolence."

"Well, one of you will need to do it, for I will be busy serving as the bait," Joel said.

"Touché," Ignacio said.

"Better," Lady Hart replied, "but not exactly there, Ignacio. We'll work on it."

"How about I do the luring," said Lady Hart, "and *you* do the conking?"

"Very well," said Joel, "I'll be the conker."

"El conquistador!" said Ignacio, "de conkerers."

"Hmm, I wonder whether 'conk' is a derivative of *conquistar*?" Lady Hart said.

"Maybe es deribateeb de conk shell?"

"You mean like someone at a meeting of the elders is passed the conk, as done in the south sea islands, and they are given the power to speak?" Lady Hart queried.

"But that would be the *opposite*, wouldn't it? If receiving the conk shell *gave* you the ability to speak, and..." Joel paused while the gears turned a few times, "...*or*, maybe, and I am just spit-balling here, but maybe 'conked out' is referring to the fact that once you *passed* the conk and you were *no longer* allowed to talk, in having been silenced you had been conked out."

"The conk shell theory is beginning to sound pretty reasonable," Lady Hart said.

"Englich saylors juse 'conk' mi amigos," Ignacio added, "et ameans *nose*. So, maybees juse punch asomebody en d'conk and dem gets knocked out."

"The nose theory works too, Ignacio," said Lady Hart. "You're on a roll, kid."

Joel looked over her fan again at the guard. "Well, this guy is not going to conk himself out," Joel said. He swatted Lady Hart in the rumpal region and said, "Now, get up there, you old woman, and distract that man."

Lady Hart carefully strolled up the short path to the privies, making sure to lift her skirts to avoid soiling them in the mud. A man passed her up and entered the outhouse just next to the outhouse protected by the guard.

"Of course he'd choose that one!" Lady Hart said under her breath. "I'll go to the..." A second man entered the outhouse just on the other side. "Seriously?" She did not know what to do but stopped next to the guard and planned to wait for one of the men to exit. The guard continued to ogle our Lady Hart.

"'Ello Miss. No need to wait, I see that there are several open outhouses," the guard said, pointing out several whose doors were slightly ajar. Several others were wide open. "Usually, we don't see any women at these privies."

"Thank you, kind sir," said Lady Hart in her best falsetto, "but I believe that I will..."

The man who had passed her on the path exited the outhouse.

Lady Hart turned and headed straight to it.

"Lady I wouldn't go in there," said the man as he passed her.

She turned and looked at the guard, who was still ogling her.

"Well," she said, "aren't you going to help me with my dress?"

The guard's eyes widened in disbelief.

She turned to enter but was halted by the stench. To keep from collapsing, she held on to the outhouse's corner and extended her right leg back, to keep from rolling backwards downhill.

Joel and Ignacio crept up behind the guard and Joel tightened his grip on the stone. He raised his arm—but the guard tripped over Lady Hart's extended right leg, which was hidden underneath the gown, toppled forward past Lady Hart into the outhouse, said "Excuse me" as he passed her, and hit his head forcefully smack dab on the hard wooden seat. He was out cold. Cold!

"Look Chole Hart, ju were awrong—he *deed* conk himself out!" Ignacio said.

Joel looked down on the man, the stone still position in the air.

"Well, that's that," said Lady Hart, "We can..."

With quickening breath, Joel unleashed a solid strike intended for the back of the man's skull, but he was not able to hang onto the stone and it left his hand, bounced off of the top of the outhouse ceiling, then the wall, and hit Joel square in the forehead. Joel stumbled back and struggled to keep his feet.

"That sounded like what I'd expect a cantaloupe to sound like were it to be struck by a stone," said Lady Hart. "Are you okay?"

"Dunno," Joel said, wiping off the splattered blood from his face with the back of his sleeve. "Maybe to make sure he was conked out I guess." He had not smiled this hard since the Tontine Coffee House.

"You didn't strike the guard, you idiot. You just let loose that stone and knocked yourself silly," Lady Hart explained.

Lady Hart bent down and grabbed the man's legs. She reminded Joel, "I'm glad that we didn't have to hurt him, I mean, he's a human being, missy," as she then heaved the man's legs over his own torso into the outhouse like they were sacks of potatoes. The man's hips rebounded to the edge of the doorway, and Lady Hart placed her foot firmly against his behind and gave it a good nudge, pushing the man's body completely inside. "A human being!"

Joel gave the guard a swift kick, though it landed making only a tiny thud, "Ow, man, that hurt."

Lady Hart shut the door. "Why the kick, kid?"

"For Tom," Joel said.

Lady Hart took a moment and then nodded with approval.

Ignacio saw a chair that was sitting between the guarded outhouse and the one now occupied by their newly conked-out foe. He took it and wedged it against the door of the outhouse.

"Good idea," said Lady Hart.

The chair came loose and tumbled ass over teakettle down the hill.

"That sucks," said Lady Hart, and then turned only to catch the last of Joel's dress disappearing into the no-longer guarded outhouse.

"Let's go," she said to Ignacio.

Together they followed Joel into the netherworld.

# 37

Lady Hart scrambled to shut the door behind her. But what if they needed to make a quick escape? She decided that the odds of avoiding being detected were best with a shut door.

She turned and moved closer behind Ignacio, who had been thrust into the lead. The tall rectangular hall cut a steeply descending path into the earth. It was surprisingly cold. Several dimly lit lanterns shimmered, set at about a foot above the ground at about five-foot intervals along each side of the hall. The tunnel seemed to be quite long. There was no staircase, but instead flat wooden planks laid lengthwise served as a kind of floor. As they made their way slowly down the ever-tilting hallway, they found underneath their feet boards that ran perpendicular across the long planks, about every two-feet, which gave them better footing and kept them from sliding all the way down. Ignacio extended his arms out to each side, using the walls of the narrow hall as guides to steady himself. His arms cast long shadows up each wall to the ceiling. Lady Hart held tightly to the fabric shoulder-pads of Ignacio's blouse. Ignacio could feel Lady Hart's breath against the back of his neck.

Suddenly, at some distance down, much further down than expected, a light appeared at the end of the long tunnel.

"Come on, you two," said the shadowy figure standing in the middle of a rectangular block of flickering light. They recognized the voice. It was Joel. He must have found a torch and lit it.

The three met at the end of the long hallway. It had taken them to what felt like a rather large room. With torch in hand, Joel led the way. The walls appeared to be littered with all sorts of primitive looking drawings. Tall spindly figures with large heads appearing to be interacting with shorter, more human looking figures. The figures appeared to gather around a large egg with legs extending to the ground. Smaller eggs with legs retracted appeared overhead, which carried what appeared to be the taller beings with big heads, some vessels glowing like small suns.

"What is all this?" asked Lady Hart.

"Beats me," Joel replied.

"I hab seen seemeelor apaintings in Meheeco," said Ignacio, "En los templos allá."

"Man, you get around," said Lady Hart.

"Jes, dat's d'good ting bout being un marinero."

"Look there," said Joel, bringing the torch closer to a place on the wall, "That looks a lot like our fortuneteller—minus the clothes and veil."

"Yes, that does look a little like her," Lady Hart confirmed.

The boys entered another hallway. They could not only hear a hum that seemed to originate from all around them but they felt a bit light-headed.

"Do you feel that?" Lady Hart asked.

"Jes," said Ignacio.

"I also hear a hum," said Joel.

"Jes, a hum también," Ignacio agreed.

They entered a very large space, how big was difficult to ascertain, but the torch's light did not reveal a ceiling. Strange, for it did not feel that they had traveled that far underground. The torch caught several shiny gold colored metal bits peeping through what looked to be something wrapped in wool blankets.

"This could be a secret Masonic Lodge," Lady Hart hypothesized. "Be careful!"

The boys approached.

The blanketed object was larger than Ignacio's uncle's ship!

Joel handed the torch to Ignacio. He took hold of the corner of one of the blankets and pulled it down. Along with it several others came crashing to the floor. The unveiling revealed a golden vessel of some type. Neither Joel nor Lady Hart had ever seen anything like it.

"I hab aseen dees sort of bessel before, amigos," said Ignacio. "It beelonges a los angeles del mar!"

"To the angles of the sea," Lady Hart whispered.

"Este es el oro que no es el oro," said Ignacio.

"Gold that is not gold," Lady Hart repeated.

The cavernous room was suddenly lit brighter. The boys turned and saw what appeared to be several men standing, holding torches with no flame. But what seemed unreal, the torches did not point upward, but in directions parallel to the floor—or wherever their holders wanted them to point. Very much like the beam of a lighthouse. Several beams landed on our three adventurers. Joel was blinded, and if he hadn't been so terrified, he would have made a run for it. But now, the three might as well have been statues chiseled out of marble.

"It's made of gold," said a young man's voice.

"Tom?" Joel said.

"Tomás?" Ignacio echoed.

The men lowered their lights. Several men split off and disappeared into the dark corridors.

It *was* Tom!

—AND THE HENCHER!

"We thought you were dead!" Joel said to Tom. Tears welled again in his eyes while he kept one eye on the hencher.

"And, had our plan worked, you would still think so," Tom said. He sounded different from before, but the same. Smarter maybe. Certainly older. He saw Joel's face. "Are you okay? You look injured."

"I'm not sure what you mean," Joel said.

"Do you work for Mister Morris and his hencher?" Lady Hart asked while starring at the hencher. "I'm not judging."

"You mean Ichtaka?" Tom said. "He does not work for Mister Morris, and he's certainly no henchman."

"We heard..."

"I am sure you have heard a lot of things," Tom said.

"But I saw him *kill* you," Lady Hart said.

"Well, you saw him *look* like he was about to—and, if we're being honest here, I think that there are times when he'd like to," Tom said with a smile looking at Ichtaka. The tall slender man grinned and let out a short grunt. But to look at him close up his eyes surprisingly expressed warmth and not a smidge of danger. "But after you fell out of the window, we were in the clear. We messed up the room a bit to make it look like a tussle."

"A heencher who is no a heencher," Ignacio said.

"Why did you do this? Why did you take me to the canal site? Was it really to protect me? From whom were you protecting me? I thought it was from *this* guy," Joel motioned at Ichtaka, "No offense." He gulped. "But why go to my father and scare the bejeezus out of him, to get him to thinking that our lives were in danger? From this guy—again, no offense. You know he could've been killed falling out of that window!" Joel paused, and then continued. "Why make us believe that we had lost you, Tom? That was very cruel, I think, and quite unnecessary." The tears rolled down his cheeks.

"So, if I may," Lady Hart interrupted, "Mister Ichtaka..."

"Just Ichtaka," Tom said.

"So, Ichtaka—great name by the way—Ichtaka does *not* work for Mister Morris?"

"Correct," Tom said.

"Are you all Freemasons or something?"

"No."

"Not going to sever our bodies in twain and all that?"

"No."

"Trabajas para el ángel del mar!" Ignacio exclaimed.

The room fell silent.

"Both Thomas and Mister Morris work for me," said Ichtaka. "I work for the angel of the sea, as you call her."

"Ichtaka is a descendant of the last emperor of the great Azteca empire, which disappeared over two centuries ago," said a man holding a bloody cloth to his forehead. "He's over a hundred and eighty years old, but to look at him you'd think maybe thirty, thirty-five tops. Lucky bastard."

"The guard!" said Joel.

"He's no guard but is in charge of this mission," said Tom. "He also works for Ichtaka."

"And you were planning to clobber this man with your stone," said Lady Hart to Joel.

"Stone?" Joel played dumb.

"The one your tiny arm let go due to the application of centripetal force which ricocheted off the interior wall of the outhouse and hit you in the melon—*that* stone," said the man. "I wasn't completely out of it—I remember the stone throwing mishap. I only wish that I had seen it."

"It was a good show, I can tell you. But...yes... good... Sir, we didn't want to hurt you; *we* didn't hurt you, which is a relief. You tripped and fell and hit your head," said Lady Hart.

"And you were very polite, I might add, for I recall your saying 'excuse me' to the lady as you plummeted headfirst into the outhouse," Joel reported.

"Jes, ju are acorrect, Señor, eet waz afer ju were a conked out dat Chole Hart a tried to conked you more out with dat stone," added Ignacio, "Right Chole Hart? Et heet heem in da cabeza like ju say. Barry funny now da I tink ob eet."

"Well, we need not elaborate, Ignacio," Lady Hart said.

"Don ju member, Ontie Hart? Ju threw hees alegs ober hees head and kicked heem into el anexo, and Chole Hart kickeded heem otra vez para Tomás! Don ju member dees tings? Creo que tus pelucas están demasiado apretadas!"

"*For Tom?*" said the man. "I recall hearing that right after feeling a light thud against my bottom. That was you?"

"They thought Ichtaka had killed me," Tom explained. "They thought that you were part of the plot."

"And why would they think that?"

"I'll explain later," Tom said with some concern.

"Tomás leeb Chole Hart at the canal to protected heem from d' hencher who is no hencher, but es a noble desandant ob de Azteca King, and den Tomás go to Ontie Hart an tell heem dat he es going to die, and he jumpeded out de weendow and almosted abroked hees neck. I finded heem en de mercado an dressed heem up like a woomans—jus like Tomás had tolded me to."

"I didn't tell him to dress them up like women," Tom clarified. "That was Iggy's doing."

"Okay, that'll do, Ignacio," Lady Hart said.

"So, that's why the two of you are dressed like that?" the man asked.

"Yes. Well, I thought that it was as a disguise," said Joel. "But to hear Ignacio tell it, sounds like we're dressed like this because of Tom. Thanks Tom!"

"Wasn't me," Tom said, "but I must admit you both look magnificent."

"Why does this Iggy call you Auntie Hart? Are you related?" the man asked Lady Hart.

"Not sure why, but it seemed appropriate all this time while in disguise. But, no, we are not related," Lady Hart answered.

"Agent Summers," the man said, "Once this is..."

"Who's Agent Summers?" Lady Hart asked looking around. "Is he invisible?"

"I am Agent Summers," said Tom. "I am Thomas Andrew Summers."

"Agent?" Joel asked.

"I am an agent for—let's call it an *agency*," he said. "We are all agents. Ichtaka has been for most of his adult life."

"Are you really over a hundred and eighty?" Lady Hart asked Ichtaka.

"One-hundred-and-eighty-seven," he said. "According to your timeline anyway. I was born in sixteen-eleven."

"You don't look a day over thirty," said Lady Hart.

"¿Cuantos años tienes, Tomás?" Iggy asked Tom.

"Thirty-three, Ignacio. I was born in seventeen-sixty-five," Tom said.

"Thirty-three?" Joel said, "I thought that you were closer to *my* age."

"According to your timeline I am thirty-three, but to mine only seventeen years have passed since my birthday. So, from *my* temporal point of view, I am seventeen, very close to your age Joel," Tom said.

"This type of work—well, the *physics* of this work—messes a bit with time," said the man. "Time has passed differently for these two relative to how it has passed for you. Let's just leave it at that."

"Wait!" Joel said, "Why are you telling us all of this? You'd only do that if you were planning to kill us."

"So you *are* Freemasons!" Lady Hart added.

The room fell silent. The words "kill us" echoed throughout the massive underground structure. A laugh could be heard coming from one of the other chambers.

"If we were going to do that, son, it would have been done," said the man. "Your unexpected visit to your 'angel,' as you refer to her, set into motion a plan that now involves the three of you. Although we cannot lay all our cards on the table—and trust me when I say that even if we did you wouldn't believe us—we need to lay enough of them out there in order to best prepare you for what we need you to do."

"Maybe after that we'll kill you," said Ichtaka. Silence. The three froze again like statues. "Oh, come on, that was funny."

"I had heard that you were a hired mercenary, formerly an Algonquin warrior," Lady Hart said.

"I heard that one too," Ichtaka said. "I greatly admire the Algonquin, but, alas, I am a warrior of the no longer existent Aztec people—well, no longer existent in this timeline anyway."

From behind the men emerged Mr. Morris, pegleg and all. "What happened to you?" he asked the man in charge.

"Assaulted by a toilet seat, I'm afraid," he said. "And apparently by those two there," motioning to Lady Hart and Joel.

Mr. Morris approached the three and extended his hand. "Pleased to finally make your acquaintance, I am Gouverneur Morris."

Joel stepped in front of Lady Hart, in cockblocking fashion, and took Mr. Morris' hand. "I know who you are, sir."

"Do you."

"We spoke with the other Mister Morris, Robert Morris, during a visit to Prune Street Prison, where he now resides. He told us a bit about you," Lady Hart said. "The kid was really taken by him. Calls him '*his giant*'."

"Don't we all," Morris replied.

Lady Hart extended her hand to Morris, "I am Ephraim Hart. It is my pleasure to meet you." Morris discarded Joel's hand and softly took Lady Hart's.

"Such soft skin, Lady Hart," Morris said.

"You know he's a man dressed in women's garb, right?" asked Joel.

"Oh, I know, Princess Joel, I know," said Morris. He turned, still holding Lady Hart's hand, and extended his free hand to Ignacio, "And you are...?"

"Ignacio López de Ayala. I am nameed ofter mi grandsfather."

Holding the hands of Lady Hart and Ignacio, Mr. Morris smiled and said, "Isn't this fun?"

Tom saw Joel staring at the mysterious lanterns.

"Interesting I know," Tom said.

"What are they?" Joel asked.

"Well, we just call it a *torch*—surprise!" Tom said.

"But there is no flame. How does it work?"

"A container of a paste-like electrolyte substance, the power source called a *battery*, produces a potential electrical current. The electricity is drawn down a metal wire, which activates a little piece of tungsten, which glows. Here let me turn it off so you can see it. Do you see it? Okay, the reflector plate, which is right there, refocuses the light and sends it outward, which is what you see here when I turn it back on."

"Why haven't I seen or heard of anything like that before?" Joel asked.

"Ordinary folks will soon enough," Tom said, "But believe it or not they have been around for some time." Tom turned to Ichtaka, "Didn't you say that the ancient Egyptians employed such devices?"

Ichtaka nodded his head. "The Olmecs did too."

"Next time you see the fortuneteller, you can ask her to tell you more about this and other marvels," Tom said.

"We will see her again?" Joel asked. An image of Frances came before his mind.

Morris suddenly stamped his pegleg hard on the floor, which created a powerful BOOM followed by a strong echo. Everyone jumped from the shock of it and stood at attention. "Goddammit, Morris," complained the man in charge with the bloodied rag still against his noggin.

"Okay, people," Morris said, "Let's get this show on the road."

# 38

The show that Mr. Morris wanted to "get on the road" involved digging the golden vessel out of the ground using the cover of night, using slave labor to do the digging, since they had no First Amendment Rights to tell the tale, transporting it to a steam-powered flat barge now waiting on the Mohawk, and moving the thing down the Hudson to New York City.

The new Federal government had plans on collecting these golden ships, which were located along the eastern coast of North America. Ichtaka knew of several more that lay entombed along the longitudinal ordinate -110.9, over all three Americas—South, Central, and North, a stretch of earth that the Aztec people knew well. Ichtaka was among many peoples who over millennia had been recruited by the fortuneteller and her sisters to protect the objects. Ichtaka was under the impression that the efforts of the fortuneteller here on Earth had been ongoing for at least two-hundred-thousand years.

Once at the port of New York, out of fear of losing the object in open waters, the vessel would be loaded onto a large flatbed, covered, and then driven by a large team of horses south to the District of Columbia, where the new Federal government was preparing to set up shop. A large temple would be constructed there to accommodate the fortuneteller. Pegleg Morris, recall, had defeated the giant Morris' potential scandal, the "Panic of 1796," which Hart and Joel had learned of during their visit to the Prune Street Prison. Pegleg Morris had been commissioned by President Washington to prepare for the move, when, in his negotiating the land sale, discovered the giant's attempt to outmaneuver Congress by secretly trying to purchase the land of the soon-to-be District of Columbia in advance and then selling it to the government for huge profits when it was ready to make the move south from Philadelphia.

The man in charge of the mission instructed Lady Hart and Princess Joel to return to the Iron Horse, clean up, get some grub, get some sleep, and await further orders. Tom volunteered to take them himself. It was a small three-man carriage, where all three—Agent, Lady, and Princess—would ride side-by-side on the driver's bench. Ichtaka rode some distance behind on horseback as security to guarantee safe passage back to Albany. Ignacio rode with Ichtaka companion-style.

Joel could hear the two talking, though they were too far back and spoke too softly for Joel to catch what they were talking about. From their cadence and tone, they seemed to be on familiar terms. What little he could ascertain from the exchange was that they were likely conversing in Spanish. Once at Albany, Hero Ignacio, Lady Hart, and Princess Joel would return to their respective abodes, while Noble Ichtaka and Agent Tom would circle back and meet up with Pegleg Morris and the man in charge of the mission.

The caravan was now midway between Cohoes and Albany.

"So, I'm not following your chain of command," said Lady Hart. "From what I can gather, everyone works for Ichtaka."

"Yes," Tom said, "we all work for him."

"But the man who toppled into the outhouse and was molested by our savage kickery claimed to be in charge."

"Well, he is in charge of *this* mission," Tom said.

"What about Morris? If I didn't know any better, I would say that *he* oversees things. You know, the pounding of his pegleg and the 'let's get this show on the road' thing? Sounded like a man in charge to me."

"Morris is in charge of extracting and moving the *object*. Once that is completed, I believe that his work here is done and he'll be off to other things," Tom said. "He works directly under Mister Bell, the man in charge. Mister Bell works directly for Ichtaka."

"Mister Bell, is it? Good. I was worried that I would have to forever refer to him as 'the man in charge'," Lady Hart said. He asked, "What does Ichtaka *do* exactly—other than look amazingly sinister?"

"That's a long story, really," Tom said.

"Is it true that he was born almost two centuries ago?" Joel asked.

"Yes, as incredible as that seems," Tom answered.

"You really seventeen?" Joel asked.

"Yes, from *my* temporal point of view, and, of course, to everyone no matter their temporal point of view, I appear seventeen, but from *your* temporal point of view I was born thirty-three years ago. To *me* I have experienced the passing of only seventeen years of life. I have not seen thirty-three years."

"Sounds downright impossible," Lady Hart said.

"It does sound impossible," Tom agreed, "it has to do with the speed of light."

"What?" Joel asked.

"Time is the measure of motion," Tom said. "Time changes depending on which motions are being measured, and whether the motion that one is measuring is accelerating or decelerating with respect to the speed of light."

"I don't follow," said Lady Hart.

"To be honest, neither do I," Tom said. "I'm sure that I've got that all wrong."

"Does the fortuneteller know?" asked Joel.

"Yes, the fortuneteller knows that and a whole lot more," Tom said. "You should ask her the next time you see her."

"Tell me one thing that she has told you," Joel pleaded.

Tom thought hard about that.

"She is from a place beyond the Moon, from the planet we call Mars."

"Mars?"

"Her people arrived there several million years ago from beyond our planetary system, from a planet in the Draco constellation," Tom said. "Now, there is an ocean-moon orbiting Saturn on which another ancient people live. They have been inhabitants of this solar system for millions of years. I am not sure where they came from. They feared the fortuneteller's people, and over several thousand years engaged in war against them. Whether an accident or an attempt to protect themselves—I'm not clear about that part—the planet between Mars and Jupiter was destroyed, which produced a dense and dangerous asteroid belt. It is still there. The asteroid belt made it almost impossible for the Saturn-Moon people to travel to Mars. Even so, several had been caught on the Mars side of the belt, and war continued. The catastrophe of the destroyed planet was so great that it was responsible for shifting the axis of the Earth. Our Moon is a fragment of that planet. The consequence of the loss of the planet was ultimately the death of Mars. Many of the fortuneteller's people who could, travelled from Mars to Earth. Like a relocated beehive or colony of ants, her people started over here on Earth."

"Sounds like a bigger version of what has happened here on this continent," said Lady Hart. "You know, the British coming here and all that..."

"Where are they, the fortuneteller's people I mean?" Joel asked.

"Not sure," Tom answered. "I get the sense that *we* are them, or at least some version of them."

"That would make sense of Kant's looks," Joel said to Hart.

"I thought we were off Kant these days," Lady Hart said to Joel.

"Kant?" asked Tom.

"Inside joke," Lady Hart said.

"I think that nature is the best teacher here," said Tom.

"What do you mean?" Joel asked.

"In one encounter with our fortuneteller, in answer to a question that I had at the time, I was taken through the metamorphosis of a dragonfly," Tom said. "It wasn't a lecture or anything like that. I *experienced* the metamorphosis *as* the dragonfly. Now I was aware of a similar cycle in the life of butterflies—you know, the change from caterpillar to butterfly?—but she emphasized the dragonfly. I asked *why the dragonfly*? And she said—well, she didn't say it in words exactly, but it was the thought—*I prefer dragonflies*."

"A reference to Draco maybe?" Joel said. "That does mean *dragon* in Latin."

"I don't know," Tom replied. "But you may be right. I hadn't made that connection. Clever. I knew I liked that about you, Joel. Anyway, where was I?"

"You were talking about *Draco* and *Dragonflies*..." Lady Hart prompted Tom.

"Yes, the dragonfly. I was surprised to learn that they spend most of their life under water. They are ferocious too. They are known to kill and eat tadpoles and even small fish," Tom said. "When a naiad is ready to undergo its metamorphosis into adult form, it stops feeding and at the darkest hour of night swims to the surface and breaks the surface of the water with its mask for the first time. Its head remains out of the water, literally out of the only world it has ever known, and into a new world it has never seen before."

"How does it breathe?" Joel asked.

"Through its anus," Tom said.

"Unexpected, I did not see that coming," said Lady Hart.

"Of course, it does begin breathing from its head during this time. The transition from anus water-respiration to mouth air-respiration is done during this phase of the transformation. Eventually, it becomes an air-breather."

"This one here enjoys a good exhale from his bottom," Joel said, motioning at Lady Hart.

"No surprise, I've seen him eat," Tom said with a chuckle, "You're funny, Joel. I also like that about you."

"You're killing me here—back to the dragonfly," said Lady Hart.

"Once the naiad can breathe, it climbs up a reed and out of the water where it attaches itself. There, when ready, it splits its exoskeleton at its back and emerges from it in adult form. Once its new exoskeleton has hardened, it takes a deep breath filling its new body, which unfolds, wings and all, completing its journey from one world to another. It no longer is a water creature. It is a creature of an entirely new element, the air."

"*We* are the dragonfly!" Joel exclaimed.

"I think so," Tom answered. "From what I understood, we are in our nymph stage, where in this life we are preparing for another world. We think that this is the only world, but it is not. We are headed to another."

"Where, I wonder?"

"I get the sense that it is beyond this three-dimensional spatial-temporal world we find ourselves in now. This world is the analogue of the water-world of the nymph. Our dragonfly lives are to be lived beyond this three-dimensional spatial-temporal world."

"Is the fortuneteller a dragonfly too?" Joel asked.

"Dunno really. But I think so. I think that we are all dragonflies—if you'll allow me to push the metaphor a bit further. She is clearly in a more advanced stage of being. She can travel between this and that next world, though she and her sisters have chosen to remain here with us until we have all crossed over."

"Sisters?"

"There are twelve fortunetellers here on Earth. I think that that's why Ichtaka refers to them as *The Guardians*. He says that the better metaphor is bees and ants—though he knows of the importance of the dragonfly story to the fortuneteller. She and her sisters are like worker bees or worker ants, he says. They care for the pupae until they emerge and assume adulthood. Our egg stage was in our primate-mother's womb. Once born, we enter the pupal stage, which is now in our full adult primate form. But we eventually shed this husk and move into the next world."

"Why primates, I wonder?" Lady Hart asked. "I'd rather be a bird or something."

"It was the closest living form on Earth to their kind, I think. Ichtaka says that the original primate they selected was modified to be able to develop and then carry a certain characteristic of *mind* or *consciousness* through the pupal stage all the way to metamorphosis. This characteristic is essential to her people, and now to us. I liken her giving to us their consciousness to the myth of Prometheus, who is said to have given human beings fire taken from the gods." Tom paused and then continued, "Death, though you and I may think of it as the end, is only our breaking free from this nymph form. We join the fortuneteller and all our ancestors in the new world, which, Ichtaka says, includes more than those of us from this Earth. Apparently, our ancestry goes back billions of years. The fortuneteller is, we might say, a very, very old cousin. Isn't that something?"

"How noble and yet how terrifying if true," Joel said. "Speaking of Greek myths, I read something about how we were once a kind of thing, an androgyne, which was a being constituted of two persons—like twins attached to one another at birth. Zeus severed us from ourselves, and now we search the world for our natural *other*. I think I see a connection to the dragonfly story that you're telling."

"Where's this? You read what where?" Lady Hart queried.

"I found a copy of Plato's *Symposium* in the reading room at the Iron Horse," Joel said. "Perhaps without really knowing it we journey in this life in search of our *other*, where this other is really just a natural expression of our instinctually seeking the next world."

"I would hope that we could find our other in *this* life," Tom said while looking into Joel's eyes.

"You know, I had always been interested in money, in thinking of people as foes to be defeated, in acquiring power for no other reason than to have it," Joel blurted out. "I called myself a capitalist."

"That doesn't sound like you," Tom said.

"Oh, believe him when he says it. I can attest to his obsession with such things," said Lady Hart. "Made us call him *The Capitalist* for a few years there."

"But this journey, meeting you, Tom, considering the bigger picture, terrified that I had lost Lady Mongoloid here, connecting with that enslaved stoic on the barge, all of it, I find that controlling resources doesn't amount to much if in the end you harm everyone else, where in harming everyone, you harm yourself. Capitalism is too brutal a system, I think. It represents more of the primate in us than anything."

"In Plato's *Republic*," Lady Hart interjected, "Socrates tells us about the man who desires to be the most powerful man in the kingdom, and in pursuing it succeeds beyond his wildest dreams at becoming the most feared but also most hated tyrant ever. But unlike the common man, who can venture out to the market by himself whenever he wants, spend time at the theater, move freely by himself anywhere he wishes, this tyrant must be guarded every minute of every day, protected by an army, for if found alone without his guard, the people would tear him to shreds! The philosophical irony is clear: by becoming the most powerful man, which you might think makes one the freest, one actually becomes the least free man in the kingdom."

"What does that have to do with...?" asked Joel.

"You know, your wanting to flourish by harming others, only to discover that by harming others you harm yourself, so you want to flourish but act so as to bring about the opposite, and all that," Lady Hart explained.

"I see. That does have to do with me. Man, this Plato really had it going. Does Socrates say that the tyrant is haunted by his pursuit of such things? I am *ashamed* of my pursuits. I don't like the idea of harming others, for what? So I can *win*? How do I win by harming others? What kind of human being am I? I look around and don't like what I see, Tom, like forcing human beings into slavery, and yet I don't..." A confused sadness overwhelmed Joel. His eyes shut tight, and his diaphragm tightened. Tears.

"I rather like this new Joel, if I'm being honest," said Lady Hart. He put his arm around Joel's shoulder and brought him close to his side. His own eyes grew heavy the moment he embraced the tiny baboon. Tears welled.

"I like this Joel, too," Tom said, giving Joel a tender nudge with his elbow. "I am grateful that I can talk about these things with someone. Thanks Joel." He put his hand on Hart's arm, "Thanks Hart."

"Say, I don't hear Ichtaka and Ignacio anymore," Joel reported as he wiped his face, using his sleeve to clean the runny nose.

"Ichtaka was going to drop Iggy off at his uncle's ship," Tom replied. "You'll see him tomorrow. You'll probably get to meet his uncle too."

"Already met. *Very* interesting man," Lady Hart yawned. "I am pooped. I haven't slept in a couple of days. And these shoes are killing me."

"You got that right, sister—these shoes *are* a pain," Joel confirmed.

"Serendipitous, then," said Tom, "we've arrived at the Iron Horse."

# 39

After following Mr. Bell's instructions, the two lay in bed. The magnificent dresses hung on the door.

"I'm gonna miss that dress," said Hart.

"I was just thinking the same thing," replied Joel.

A rumbling of the voices of what sounded like several men arose behind the door. Underneath shadows were cast onto the floor reaching into their room. A powerful knock!

"Mister Hart," said a voice. A second round of knocks. "Mister Hart."

"Oh my," Hart whispered to Joel. "Who is that?"

"I dunno," Joel said. "Answer it."

"Mister Hart?" said the voice.

"Sounds like the Sheriff," Joel said.

"The Sheriff?" Hart cried. He got out of bed and opened the door. "Yes, Sheriff."

The Sheriff stood in the doorway flanked by two Deputies. Joel recognized one of them. Behind them, trying to see between their wide frames, was Mr. Wrench.

"I told you they were in there," said Mr. Wrench.

"May we come in?" asked the Sheriff.

"Why of course, Sheriff," Hart said.

Mr. Wrench brought in two oil lamps that illuminated the room.

"How did you know it was the Sheriff?" asked the Sheriff.

Hart turned and looked at a lump under the blankets. The Sheriff now understood.

"Mister Hart I am Sheriff Brown and these are two of my Deputies, Johnson and Johnson—Don't say it. You know Mister Wrench."

"Yes, thank you, Sheriff Brown," Hart said. He shook each Deputy's hand, "Johnson...Johnson."

The Sheriff looked at the lump under the blankets. He smiled. "Hello Joel, I see you there."

Joel slowly pulled the blankets back. "Hello Sheriff, Deputies Johnson, Mister Wrench."

"You had us worried, young man," the Sheriff said.

"Yeah, sorry about that," Joel said, "But please believe me when I say that it wasn't my intention."

"I am happy to see that your father is alive and well," Sheriff Brown said.

The Sheriff turned to Mr. Wrench. "Deputies would you please excuse us and man the door?"

"Yes, Sheriff," said one of the Johnsons.

"I'll need you to step out, too, Mister Wrench," the Sheriff said.

"But I..."

The Sheriff gave Mr. Wrench a stern look. Mr. Wrench backed out of the room. One of the Johnsons helped Mr. Wrench clear the door and softly shut it.

"Thank you, Mister Wrench," the Sheriff said through the door, and then he turned to Hart and Joel. "Gentlemen, you put us through quite the ringer these past few days."

"I'm so sorry Sheriff..." Joel said.

The Sheriff held up his hand, indicating that he wanted Joel to stop talking, and with the other he reached into his coat pocket and pulled out an envelope along with a small case. He handed Joel the case and asked Joel to get from it his reading glasses. The Sheriff took his time to unfold an already torn envelope and pulled from it a letter. Joel unfolded the wire spectacles. The Sheriff reached out and took them from Joel and put them on. He then looked at the letter, at Hart and Joel, and then back at the letter.

"What's this?" Hart asked.

"It's a letter, Mister Hart," said the Sheriff.

"Well, I know it's a letter," Hart replied. "I meant, what does it have to do with us?"

The Sheriff read it aloud, though only loud enough for the three of them to hear:

To the Honorable Gordon Earl Brown, Sheriff of Albany County. It has come to our attention that two citizens have recently acquired your services as the chief law enforcement officer of the County. They are a Mr. Ephraim Hart and a Mr. Joel Hart. The Attorney General of the United States of America has extended to each Federal protection. We so order that you do not inquire into their current work, and surrender them to Mr. Gouverneur Morris, a Representative of the Department of War, who will meet you at the Iron Horse 0600 Monday, October 24, 1798.

"It arrived late this afternoon," said Sheriff Brown. He turned the letter around so that both could see it. "It's signed by The Attorney General of the United States and the Secretary of War."

"It is," said Hart. "Imagine that. Monday is tomorrow?"

"Now, I'm not sure what the two of you are up to, but since I am not supposed to ask, let me just say that I am happy that the both of you are safe, and that I can take this case, or whatever it was, off my list of things to concern myself about," the Sheriff said.

"So, we will just join Mister Morris tomorrow morning, then?" Joel asked.

"That's what the letter says," the Sheriff replied. "I will leave one of the Deputies here tonight, and I'll come by in the morning to surrender the two of you into Mister Morris' custody."

"Sheriff, I don't think that we need protection," Joel said. "The tall man with tattoos on his face turns out to be a good man. Mister Morris works for him."

"I'll come by in the morning to surrender the two of you into Mister Morris' custody," the Sheriff repeated.

"He has a pegleg," Hart added.

"A pegleg. Very good, Mister Hart," said Sheriff Brown.

He turned to exit and got a good look at the dresses hanging on the door. "He told me that you two came in wearing dresses, Mister Wrench that is, but I didn't believe him."

"Sheriff," Joel said. "When you spoke with me in the dining room, you told me that Tom's body was up here in the room—dead. You said that I had to wait for the Undertaker and Magistrate to remove the body before I could go back to my room."

"Tom's not dead?" the Sheriff said with a grin.

"So, you know what this is about?" Joel asked.

"Some of it, young man. Only some of it," the Sheriff said. "A need-to-know situation. But I know enough to keep me up some nights. I know enough to know that your tattooed man is no Indian."

Sheriff Brown exited the room.

"Can you believe that?" asked Hart.

"This is turning out to be some adventure," said Joel.

"You're telling me, kid."

# 40

The clock in the hall rang out five bells. Hart came to and nudged Joel. "Get up you little baboon."

Hart went out and brought back a pitcher of warm water from the kitchen. "The Deputy is still out there," he said. He poured a bit of the warm water into a large porcelain bowl and washed his face and neck. "I'm not going to shave today. I want to be a little rugged when we see Morris. Do you see this mustache coming in. Do you see it?" He rinsed off, patted his face and neck with a towel, and saw the dress.

"You can't keep it," Joel said, "it belongs to Ignacio."

Hart took down the dress from where it was hanging on the door and stood before the long mirror in the room, holding the dress in front of him. He admired the way it brought out his ever-so-subtle tanned complexion and burgeoning mustache. "Debería haber sido maniero," he said aloud. "Podría usar vestidos todo los dias!"

"You learned all that Spanish from just one night on the ship?" Joel asked.

"No. It all kind of came to me after seeing the fortuneteller," Hart explained.

"We need to get a move on here. The Goove will be here soon," Joel said.

"The Goove—good one!" Hart said.

They did their best to fold the dresses and put them along with their borrowed shoes into the bag, the bag that Ignacio had given to Joel, the one in which he had received the dress and shoes. It was large enough to accommodate both of Ignacio's festive equator-dresses. The shoes made the bag a bit heavy.

"I suppose we won't have time for breakfast," Hart said.

"Maybe the kitchen staff can drum something up," Joel replied.

A knock.

Hart opened the door. It was the Deputy with a small tray that had two cups of coffee and two small plates on which sat eggs and bacon and toast. A spoon's worth of strawberry jam adorned each plate.

"Mister Wrench wanted you to have this," said the Deputy.

"How thoughtful," said Hart as he took the tray from the Deputy. "Would you like a bite?"

"No thank you. I'll have breakfast once the Sheriff arrives." He stared at the bacon for a second longer and then said, "Well, that may be a while," and took a strip of bacon from the plate. "Thank you," he said.

"You're welcome," Hart replied and softly shut the door.

"That was nice of Mister Wrench," Joel said.

"I wonder whether Mister Wrench knows of all this?" Hart asked.

"I doubt it. Seems pretty secret and all," Joel replied.

"The Sheriff hinted that he knows a little about what's going on," Hart said. "Can you believe that letter from the US Attorney General and Secretary of War?"

"I know, right?" Joel said. "I figure that the Sheriff knows a lot more than he's letting on."

"What do you think of Ichtaka, now that we know a little more about him?"

"I think he's dreamy," Joel said.

"Better not let Tom hear you say that. He might get jealous," Hart cautioned.

"You're hilarious," Joel retorted. "I cannot tell you how happy I was to see Tom again."

"I know. I felt the same."

"What do you think happens next?" Joel asked.

"No sé mi pequeño babuino. But it looks like it's going to be really something!"

A loud thud came from behind the door. It shook the wooden floor beneath their feet. The two looked at one another and Joel went to the door and slowly opened it. The Deputy lay on the ground. He was not breathing!

"Oh my," said Hart, "what has happened?"

They looked at each other and then at the tray of food on the nightstand.

# 41

Chaos set upon the Iron Horse. Several guests on the second floor had now come out of their rooms and hovered over the body of Deputy Johnson. Others ran out from the sitting and dining rooms into the foyer.

All jumped when they heard a scream from downstairs.

A man entered the foyer from the kitchen, stopped and posed as though an announcer at a regal ball.

"Mister Wrench is dead!" shouted the well-posed man.

"Dead?" screamed Hart. Everyone turned and looked at him standing with his hands hiding his mouth.

"The Deputy up here is dead also!" shouted a man standing next to Joel.

Sheriff Brown and several of his men entered the front door. He appeared shaken. "You say the Deputy is dead?"

"Yes Sir, Sheriff, dead as a doornail," shouted the man who had just shouted.

"Doornails are not the sorts of things that *can* be dead," said Hart quietly to Joel, "It's just a conceptual matter. A category mistake if I ever saw one."

"I think that you are retreating to your philosophical safe place," Joel diagnosed.

"You got that right," Hart said. "What is going on?"

"Mister Wrench is dead, too," the man downstairs said to the Sheriff.

"Wrench dead too?"

"Dead as a doornail."

"Seriously?" shouted Hart.

The Sheriff told several of his men to go to Mr. Wrench and then ran up the stairs all along looking for the body on the floor.

"We didn't do it," Joel said to Sheriff Brown.

"I think that it was the bacon," Hart shouted.

"Bacon?" asked the Sheriff confused.

"Yes, your Deputy brought us up breakfast and he said that Mister Wrench had instructed him to bring it up, and I asked him if he wanted a bite, and he said no, but was eyeing my bacon, and then said you were probably going to be while longer and took a piece of bacon because of the being-a-while-longer thing. A few moments went by and—thud!" Hart shouted.

"You need to calm down," Joel said to Hart.

"Calm down!?!" shouted Hart, his hands moving to cradling both sides of his crown.

"No one touch the bacon," the Sheriff commanded.

"I'm not touching none of it," said someone in the crowd.

The Sheriff knelt beside the body and closed the Deputy's eyelids. "Real shame. Johnson was a good man."

A Deputy made his way up the stairs. "Sheriff," he said, "The cooks think that it was the bacon. Say it may have been poisoned. It was right after eating a strip that Mister Wrench and the dog became stiff and just fell flat. Mitchell shut his eyelids if that was okay."

"The dog's?"

"No, Sir, sorry...Mitchell's. Johnson shut 'em, Sir—the other Johnson, of course, not the dead one up there with you."

"Will no one shut the dog's eyes?" cried Hart. "This is madness!"

"Deputy," said the Sheriff, "round up the guests and bring them to the dining room. Make sure no one eats anything."

"Yes, sir," said the Deputy.

"Can we eat the eggs and toast?" asked someone from the dining room.

"What did he say?" asked the Sheriff.

"He wants to know if he can eat the eggs and toast," shouted a Deputy from the foyer.

"No!" the Sheriff returned.

"I already ate breakfast, bacon included!" said a woman in the foyer.

"How do you feel?" asked a man.

"Fine. I feel fine," she said.

Joel and Hart were about to go downstairs with the others when the Sheriff looked up. "You two hold off. Please go back to your room and wait for me."

"This is all for real, right Sheriff?" Joel asked. "It's not like the Tom thing is it?"

"No, young man, I'm afraid that this one is the real thing," said the Sheriff.

At the front door appeared Mr. Bell and Mr. Morris. Tom followed. Joel could see Ignacio outside minding the horses.

Joel waved to Tom, but he didn't see Joel. He and Hart then went back into their room. Hart left the door partially open so that he could see what was happening. Mr. Morris and Tom came upstairs and stood with the Sheriff. The three of them stared at the body on the floor.

"Is it what we think it is?" asked Mr. Morris.

"It may be what you think it is," replied the Sheriff.

"Ominous if so," said Mr. Morris.

"Ominous indeed," said the Sheriff. "Looks like he got to Wrench too."

"I heard," said Mr. Morris. He went back downstairs to the foyer.

"We'll see to it, Sheriff, that he'll pay for what he has done here," said Tom.

"See to it, then," said the Sheriff. "I'll swing by Johnson's place this morning and tell his wife that she's a widow."

"What are they talking about?" Hart whispered to Joel.

"Beats me," Joel replied, "But it sounds like they know who did this."

Tom's face appeared in the empty space between the doorjamb and door. Joel and Hart jumped back.

"Good morning, you two," Tom said. "I will explain this later. We need to get you out of here." He turned to the Sheriff. "Sheriff, I will take these two with me downstairs. We need to skedaddle them out of here pronto."

"I understand, Agent Summers," the Sheriff said.

Tom turned to Joel and Hart. "Get your things," he said.

They gathered up the bag full of dresses and shoes.

"The trunk!" Joel said to Hart.

"Too heavy for me," Hart said.

"Tom," said Joel, "what should we do about the trunk?"

"Leave it here. You won't be needing it where we are going."

"Where are we going?" asked Joel.

"Downstairs and to the carriage outside," Tom replied.

"No, I mean where are we going going?"

"Don't worry about that now. I'll arrange to have your trunk brought to you," Tom said. "But we need to go now."

They exited the room carrying the bag of dresses. Mr. Morris saw them from downstairs in the foyer.

"Hey you two," he sang with a big smile and gave an even bigger wave and then stomped his pegleg twice on the floor.

"Man, that'll never stop being creepy," Hart said to Joel.

# 42

They arrived back at the outhouses in Cohoes. Ichtaka stood on a small hill behind the privies.

"I don't recall that hill being there," Hart said.

"It's from last night's dig," Tom replied.

The carriage stopped and the five of them exited. Ignacio handed off the reins to a new driver who headed back in the direction of the town.

"So you dug up that golden ship?" Hart asked.

"We did indeed," Mr. Morris interjected.

As they walked up the hill to Ichtaka they could see a deep hole in the ground. Their feet sunk slightly into the dirt that constituted the new hill.

A tall wooden A-frame stood over the hole. Men were pulling ropes that lifted out of the hole large rectangular objects that were wrapped in wool blankets.

"What are those?" Joel asked.

"The men have been chiseling out the walls piece by piece—those sections that had the drawings on them.

"I remember those," Hart said.

"They will be delivered to their new home in the Federal city," added Tom.

"Is it true?" Ichtaka asked Mr. Bell.

"Yes, it is," he said.

"We must be very careful," said Ichtaka, "He could be anyone anywhere." The two turned from the group to get some privacy and continued their conversation.

"What are they talking about?" Joel asked Tom.

"There is someone who worked with the fortuneteller, not a human being like us, but is not from Mars either. It, though we refer to it as a *he*, can travel time, can move between dimensions, and can shapeshift..."

"Shapeshift?" Joel asked.

"He is able to take on the forms of living things—appearing to be a wolf, a bear, an elk, a dog, a snake, or a man," Tom said.

"That's terrifying!" Hart said.

"Terrifying for sure," Tom said.

"Ichtaka says that the shapeshifter was a captive of the fortuneteller's people," Tom said.

"He is from the Saturn-Moon world?" asked Joel.

"That's my understanding," Tom said. "They are a reptile-looking people when not shapeshifting."

"Interesting," said Joel, "my impression of the fortuneteller is that she looks a little like a praying mantis."

"Interesting. She looked a little like that to me, too," Hart interjected.

"You were saying about the reptile man..." Joel prompted Tom.

"After several millennia bound and imprisoned on our Moon, he escaped and made his way here to Earth."

"Why can't he return to his world?" Hart asked.

"Not sure," Tom said. "It was after the fortuneteller's people moved to modify the primates here in order to secure their own survival, he began his work to destroy the experiment. He's a slippery one since he can apparently cloak himself so as to go undetected by the sisters when not in our three-dimensional world."

"He sounds like *Satan* in Milton's poem *Paradise Lost*," Joel said.

Tom looked at him in a way that confirmed the insight. "The connection that initially struck me was *Set*, a god of ancient Egypt, or *Akuma* of the ancient far east stories. But the connection to Satan has crossed my mind more than once."

"Why doesn't he just kill everyone and be done with it?" Joel asked.

"The sisters constantly search for him, and if he shows himself in our three-dimensional world for more than a few minutes they are alerted to him. Remember they also exist outside of our three-dimensional world. To continue, he can do only so much damage at any given time. At some point he will be destroyed."

"So you think that he is responsible for what happened this morning?" Hart asked.

"Yes," Ichtaka interjected. "As you no doubt have surmised, he was after you two. Mister Wrench and Deputy Johnson were unfortunate casualties of this ongoing war."

"Don't forget the dog," Hart added.

Ichtaka continued staring at the large, wrapped objects being pulled out of the ground.

"Say, how do we know that he isn't one of *us*?" Hart asked. "Well, not one of us, I mean, but is pretending to be one of us?"

"We don't really," Tom said. "But wait a few minutes. If he's here, Ichtaka would be alerted, and he'd do what he has been trained to do."

"To look awesome even if just staring into that hole?" Hart said.

"Don't be so glib," Joel said.

"I'm not being glib, kid—this is me being *wigged out*."

"I can relate," said Mr. Morris. "Now, I must get off this hill, my pegleg keeps threatening to sink into the dirt up to the knee. He smacked Hart hard enough on the hinny to lift him off his feet. "Ladies, the barge awaits," he sang and then hopped down the hill on one leg.

# 43

The flat barge was much larger than the one used to transport workers back and forth between Albany and Cohoes. On it sat what appeared to be a very large boat wrapped in blankets, the blankets secured by a system of ropes. The thing looked like one big grey birthday present.

"How did you get it on the barge? It looks heavy," Joel asked. "I mean, if it is gold, I'm surprised that it didn't sink the barge."

"*Lots* of manpower and several machines," said Mr. Morris.

"The materials out of which the ship is made are odd that way. It's covered in gold, but the ship is not made completely of gold. Incredibly strong but light," added Tom.

Joel noticed that the density of workers in the camp was considerably less than it was when he was there last. Most notable was the scarcity of black men moving about. Not anything like before.

"What manpower?" asked Hart. "The place looks almost deserted."

"The majority of slave labor left on barges last night, the last of them embarking earlier this morning, before dawn," Tom said. "The rest are on foot. Since we didn't pass any on the road, looks like they had made it south of Albany before we set out."

"What about the state prisoners?" asked Joel.

"They are still somewhere in the camp," Tom said. "I think that we were looking at several there who were working the ropes at the hole. But they are scheduled to disperse and to return to a network of state prisons this afternoon."

Men were loading the large rectangular hunks of the wall onto the deck of the barge.

"Does that do it for the Western Inland Lock Navigation Company, then?" asked Hart.

"I think so, my Mister Hart," said Morris. "I do miss you in that dress, I might add."

"Thank you," Hart replied, "I was telling Joel this morning how much I'm going to miss that dress."

"Te lo puedo vender si quieres," said Ignacio.

"Gracias, Ignacio, podría aceptarte en eso," Hart said.

"Your father has really blossomed Spanish-wise," said Tom to Joel. "Having a mastery over languages seems to be common among those who have encountered the fortuneteller."

"I know," Joel said, "But from what I can tell, nothing like that rubbed off on me. Do you have any idea what my fatherly baboon said?"

"Ignacio said that he would sell the dress to your father if he liked, and your father thanked him and said that he might just take him up on the offer," Tom explained.

"Tell him that he doesn't have the money to buy such things," Joel said to Tom.

"Señor Hart," said Tom, "tu hijo dice que no tienes el dinero."

"Now that the Western Inland Lock Navigation Company is kaput," Hart replied, "tengo el dinero!"

Tom turned to Joel and reported, "He said..."

"I got the drift of it," Joel interrupted. He was reminded that they still had to find a stockjobber who would sell them stock so that they could return it to Mr. Carmichael. He also thought that he and Hart would have to do something that would square things with Carmichael, since they had initially set out to use him as a means to a corrupt end. Even Kant would say that one should never use another human being as solely a means to an end, whether corrupt or not. Of course, Kant would probably want us to steer clear of corrupt ends. Stupid Kant, Joel thought with an internal smile, the wigged pigman looked to be onto something important after all.

Ichtaka and his cadre of helpers boarded the barge—Ignacio, Hart, and Joel now included. They found several serious looking armed infantrymen already posted on the barge, rifles at the ready.

# 44

Joel could see the outline of the Port of Albany. Ships looked to be crossing into what was clearly their lane, though the captain did not seem concerned.

"Don't worry," the captain said to Joel, "they're at least a mile away. By the time we get to where they are now positioned, they'll be clear of us."

Joel looked at the captain and smiled.

The barge took only forty-minutes to make its way from Cohoes to Albany.

"Hey, do you need to use the privy before we hit port?" asked Hart.

"What?" Joel said.

"The privy."

"They have a privy onboard?" Joel asked.

"Not just one, it's a bench that runs the width of the entire barge. It's located at the stern," Hart said while pointing to the back of the boat. "You just go back there, take your pants down, sit over one of the holes in the bench, and fire away right into the Hudson."

"Gross," said Joel.

"Not gross at all," Hart replied, "rather invigorating. And, as a plus, you get to go with a number of others. A real social event."

"I don't need to go," Joel said, "But thanks for the information."

"De nada, mi hijo," Hart replied.

Ignacio appeared. "Hey, deed ju try d'preevies ot d'stern?" he asked. "Barry leeberating."

Ignacio and Hart laughed. Joel stood his stoic ground.

Mr. Morris approached from the stern buckling his pants, "Young man, do you..."

"By the gods, were *all* of you back there pooping?" Joel asked.

"There were a lot more than the three of us I can tell you," Mr. Morris said. "Several are still back there if you want to get in on it."

"Is there anyone else who wants to talk about the pooper in the back?" Joel shouted.

"There's a pooper at the *stern*?" corrected a voice from what was very likely the pooper at the stern.

Several men laughed—including the infantrymen.

Tom approached from the bow.

"Good," said Joel, "someone who has *not* been at the stern pooping."

"I pooped right after we got underway," Tom said. "Why do you need to go?"

Joel looked away. Everyone finally fell silent about the pooping and were drawn to the trees on the bank. It was a spectacular early fall day. The slow rise and fall of the deck quickly calmed all nerves.

Joel could hear the wheels on each side of the barge exiting the river, which brought water up along with its paddles, the water raining down on the deck. It sounded almost like what he imagined a Moorish fountain would sound like.

"Hey," Tom said to Joel, "we need to talk."

"I am going to miss you and Ignacio," Joel said. "Sorry, but I needed to say that straight out of the gate."

"What if you didn't have to—miss us, I mean?"

"What do you mean?"

A heavy pause.

"Ichtaka believes that you two would make strong additions to our effort."

"He does?"

"The fortuneteller was taken by you," Tom said, "And Ichtaka agrees with her assessment."

"I don't know," Joel said, "I'm not sure that Hart would be up for it. My mother. I don't think that he could part with her. He hasn't shown it, but I think he really misses her."

"Hart isn't invited," Tom said.

A heavier pause.

"But you said 'you two,'" Joel said.

"I was referring to you and Ignacio," Tom explained. "Your mother is already on her way back. Your grandfather died several weeks ago," he added.

"She is? He did? How do you...?" Joel said, "Hart and I will need to be home when she arrives."

"Hart will need to be home. A fork in the road you have been on has now presented itself, Joel."

"A fork in the road?"

"You can continue and return with Hart, or..."

"...Or what?," Joel asked.

"You can join us—well, join *me*, I mean—on a once in a lifetime adventure."

"Join *you*?"

"We can be together for the rest of our lives, while we exist in *this* form, before we undergo metamorphosis and become dragonflies. And I see no reason to think that we couldn't continue together in that new world. You remember the story?"

"Something about that sounds oddly right to me," Joel confessed as he recalled fragments of a vision he had during his encounter with the fortuneteller. He focused. "And Ignacio too?"

"Ignacio too," Tom said.

Joel's eyes looked downward. His chin dropped a bit.

"What is it?" Tom asked.

"I'm afraid to say it."

"Say it, Joel, I want to hear it."

"I thought...Tom, this is hard...I don't want you to hate me...but..." He took a breath. "But I thought that when you were saying just now that we would be together that you meant *together*—you know, like together together." He lowered his voice to a whisper, "Like love and all that." He lowered his head and squeezed his face as if trying to hide it from view.

After a few seconds of awaiting Tom's rejection but hearing nothing, Joel lifted his eyes and found Tom's. Tom was calm and approving.

"I did mean together together Joel. I loved you the moment I saw you." He reached into his satchel and pulled from it a book. "I was going to give this to you later, but now seems like the right time." He handed it to Joel.

It was Plato's *Symposium*!

Joel looked to see if anyone had heard what Tom had said. But the others were caught up in some story that Mr. Morris was telling. He could feel an intense pressure in his forehead right behind his eyes. His face grew hot. His heartbeat filled his entire body. It was like he was a stringed instrument, and someone had plucked him good. The heat and pressure calmed, and the pluck now vibrated a kind of joy that he had never felt before.

"I saw you reading it in the reading room that Friday, through the window as I was leaving," Tom explained. "When you were at dinner I returned, wanting to see what had captivated you so. I found the hair you had placed in it. I read the passage it marked. That's when I knew I could tell you."

"I feel like I'm in a dream," Joel said. "But you said that Ignacio was coming with you too. So I just assumed that you meant that we'd be together, you know, as friends."

"Ignacio has his own path. My relationship with him will be very different from the one I hope to have with you. But the three of us *will* be great friends. I'm sure of that!"

Joel opened the book and looked through its pages. "Did you steal this?"

"No, I bought it from Wrench. Said he was happy to free up space on the top shelf." He paused, then added, "I kept the hair of course."

"Really?"

"No. That'd be weird," Tom laughed, reaching out and plucking a hair from Joel's head, "why keep the one when there's plenty more where that came from?"

"What will Ignacio think of *us*, I mean of our being together together?"

"He is much more experienced, much wiser than you and I and I've found him to be open to multiple ways of being human. If anyone has transcended social mores, it's him. That's one of his strengths that attracted both the fortuneteller and Ichtaka to him. He will be happy for us. I mean, just look at him, he's Iggy!"

Joel looked at Ignacio laughing with Hart, the two arm in arm.

"He really *is* great," Joel admitted.

Joel and Tom watched Mr. Morris as he picked up the dress-filled bag sitting on the deck and ask Ignacio. "This is yours I take it?"

"Jes, ju take et aright, Meester," Ignacio humorously confirmed.

"May I?" Morris asked.

"O cours, Meester Morris," Ignacio said.

Morris produced one of the wigs from the bag. "Oh my, this is wonderful." He began to put it on. "Ow!" he shouted. "What on earth?" He pulled from the wig a long-pointed, pale object.

"Thot's Chole Hart's askeenny mysterious whale bone, Señor," Ignacio said. "The fortuneteller gibbed it to heem. Do not a steal it," he said with a laugh.

"Well it stung me good," said Morris. "Did it draw blood?" he asked as he gave his hand to Ignacio to inspect.

"No, ju are good."

Morris put on the wig. "Does anyone have a mirror?"

"I have one in my trunk," Hart said. "But we left that back at the Iron Horse."

Morris put the wig back into the bag and gave the bag to Ignacio. His demeaner changed immediately after that, looking like he had done something that he didn't want anyone to know he did—the sort of look one gets after having silently farted in mixed company. That sort of look.

But Joel's attention was immediately drawn back to Tom and to their conversation.

"What will I tell Hart?" Joel asked. "That Kantian and I have been companioning pretty much my entire life."

"Tell him the truth," Tom said. "He knows what love is. He'll understand. He's a good man." Tom then changed his voice, mimicking what he remembered a parent sounding like, "Besides, you're a man now, bound to eventually leave home. Your destiny is calling you young man." He looked for Joel's reaction at his lame attempt at comedic relief. "Please consider it," he said softly.

Joel looked away and caught Hart's eyes and Hart knew at that very moment that he would never see Joel again. Tears welled up. A smile. He recalled something like this being shown to him when encountering the fortuneteller, something that he had forgotten or maybe repressed. Joel tried with his glance to apologize, to explain, but the encounter would only allow for the realization of their parting and promise of a brief period of sorrow. Hart's face softened and his smile grew longer as though to say to Joel that he understood and that it was okay for him to go with Tom. The two halves of an androgyne had found each other. How joyful and comforting. He couldn't wish for anything better for his son.

Ichtaka watched the encounter between them from a distance. "The boy has decided to come," he said to an internal companion. "It is good," a voice replied.

# 45

The captain ordered that the starboard wheel be slowed to seventy percent. Immediately the barge began to slowly veer to the right, toward the dock. A bell rang and the captain then ordered that the starboard wheel be brought back to full speed. The barge began to slowly align with the downriver current again. Once parallel to the dock, though at least twenty yards away, the captain ordered that the wheels come to full stop and then to reverse rotation "to bring it even," he said.

"What is he doing?" asked Hart.

"Hees going to rotate d'wheels so dat d'barge no longer goes downriver," said Ignacio.

"So we'll just stay steady here at *this* location?" asked Hart.

"Jes," Ignacio said.

The barge seemed to mysteriously stay in one place relative to the dock. It produced an odd feeling for those on the barge who had gotten used to the sensation of moving relative to the banks of the Hudson.

"Aren't we going to dock?" asked Hart.

"No...look!" said Tom.

A large dingy rowed by two men was now working from the dock out to the barge. A tall dark man with a black beard and moustache that made him look like a fierce buccaneer stood at the boat's bow.

"Tío?" Ignacio said.

It *was* Ignacio's uncle—the captain of the large schooner, which had remained in port all this time but now looked like it was about to get underway.

The dingy reached the barge and a boatswain threw the fierce-looking captain a long portion of a heavy rope. He snatched it out of the air without even looking and pulled the dingy close to the barge with it. He gave the rope to one of the rowers, and the boatswain reached out, took the captain's forearm, and together they worked to bring the captain onboard. Ignacio's uncle was almost as tall as Ichtaka.

"Tío," Ignacio cried. "Gracias por viene!"

They faced-off.

"Ven," the captain said in a stern voice. He opened his arms.

Ignacio raced to his uncle, and they embraced tightly. Those on the barge were warmed by the intense emotion radiating from the captain's face. He looked to be crying. He reared back to get a good look at Ignacio, cradling his nephew's face with both hands, searching for the Ignacio who lay hidden in his eyes. Ignacio's body shook.

"Has sido un hijo para mi," the captain said.

"You have been a son to me," Hart translated.

"Lo sé y has sido un padre para mi," Ignacio replied.

"I know, and you a father to me."

"Honra a tus antepasados," the captain said.

"Honor your ancestors."

"Los honraré mi padre," Ignacio whispered.

"I shall honor them, my father."

"Nos vemos en el otro lado," the captain said.

"I shall see you on the other side."

"Sí, ven a buscarme," Ignacio responded.

"Yes, come find me," Hart whispered.

He shoved Ignacio as though completing an initiation ritual, making the separation final. He looked at those who were watching and stopped dead when locating Joel. His powerfully penetrating stare stunned Joel as though Joel had accidentally caught a glimpse of the Medusa herself.

Ichtaka stood before Hart.

Joel's heart pounded.

"It is time," Ichtaka said to Hart. He looked at Joel, "Say goodbye to your father."

Hart turned to Joel. Hart was trembling. Joel was saddened to see him so vulnerable. He now understood the fulness of Pausanias' great speech about a heavenly love shared between men. That love was what he and Hart now radiated. Hart straightened himself and took Joel in his arms and they both squeezed tighter than they ever had. They wept, along with several others onboard, including the heavily armed infantrymen.

"Goodbye, my old baboon," Joel whispered. He stroked Hart's hair. "I will miss you."

"I will miss you," Hart whispered back. "I will tell your mother that you have taken a position with an international trade company or something."

"Make sure that Uncle Yusuf thinks that I am bringing in the coin." He laughed with tears running down his cheeks. He paused and looked at Hart's face hoping to remember every detail, and then said, "Take care of each other, Hart. I know that she loves you deeply."

Ichtaka placed his strong hand on Hart's shoulder and together they walked to meet Ignacio's uncle who had been waiting. The fierce-looking buccaneer smiled warmly at Hart and then took Hart's hand. The two faced the crew, faced their *sons* one last time, and together they turned away and the captain leapt into the dingy, turning to assist Hart as he slowly made his way from the barge. The captain threw the rope back to the boatswain and the dingy slowly moved away from the barge. It turned toward the dock, and the rowers powered the dingy toward shore. Neither father looked back.

"Ignacio's uncle will take your father home," Tom said. "His trunk has already been brought to the ship." He put his arm around Joel's shoulder and then motioned to Iggy to come. The three of them embraced and wept. They were children no longer. An end had come. A *good* end. But as with every ending there is a new beginning. Nature is our best teacher. The dragonflies—remember the story?

The captain of the barge then ordered that the wheels be stopped and together brought full speed forward. They were now headed to the Port of New York City. From there, only the fortuneteller could know for sure.

Milton Keynes UK
Ingram Content Group UK Ltd.
UKHW010730241123
433194UK00001B/109